Where the Bluegrass Grows

Equestrian Romance Series – Book 1

Laurie Berglie

ISBN-13: 978-1523285044
ISBN-10: 1523285044

Cover Photo Credit: Mary Jane Speer
Cover Design Credit: La Familia Media

For James –
Thanks for not only pushing me to finish this, my first novel, but for being a constant inspiration. I love you.

~ Chapter 1 ~

When fiction writer Molly Sorrenson realized her real life was starting to read like one of her novels, she knew it was time for a break.

It was nine-thirty at night and another bad first date was in the books. *Sorry*, Molly thought, *but if you're going to take four calls on your cell before drinks and appetizers are served, it's not going to work.* She sat politely through the meal anyway, skipped coffee and dessert, and left as soon as she could get away. Her friends meant well, but no more blind dates.

As she sat at her desk, a worn cherry-wooded Shaker style with drawers on each side, she reflected on the last few months of her life. Her latest novel had hit the stands to above average success, but her love life had taken a turn for the worse. She had left Ty, her longtime love, after she found incriminating text messages linking him with a younger, blonder co-worker. And while she had teared up as she watched him pack up his cologne and toothbrush, and briefly had one small moment of weakness when she wanted to chase him down the sidewalk before he jumped into his Range Rover, she bit her lip and let him go. Breaking up with him had been the right decision, however, as she recently found out through a mutual friend that Blondie the Co-worker was pregnant.

The news scorched her like wild fire does the dry earth, but she knew she was better off without him. Though he had never treated her poorly, she sometimes felt that there had been something missing in their relationship, but she could never quite pinpoint what it was. Thinking about it now, Molly figured that she and

Ty probably stayed together for as long as they had simply because it had been easy, and change, even if for the better, is hard.

Molly's novel had been the only bright spot on the horizon; at least she still had her career. Her third novel, *So This Is It*, was much in line with her first two, a little romance, a few conflicts, an overall nice story. Some described her work as "chick lit," but she didn't care. She was able to make a living off her writing, one of two true passions in her life, and she was satisfied.

Having grown up on her parents' farm in Monkton, Maryland, it made sense that her other passion was horses. There are numerous pictures of Molly and her older sister, Erin, sitting astride their fat Shetland pony, Sundance, smiling for the camera and looking as happy as could be. With her chestnut coat and flaxen mane and tail, Sunny, as they called her, was absolutely adorable, the perfect children's pony. Molly was barely two years old when she would run out to find Sunny grazing in her field, cling to her legs, and plant kisses on her nose. Molly learned to ride soon thereafter and never looked back.

Her parents still live on their farm, and Molly loves that she is only a few miles down the road. Four years ago, at the age of twenty-five and high on her first book deal, Molly finally exerted some independence and moved into a neighbor's carriage house. Small, but open and airy, the carriage house she rented boasted one bedroom, a patio that overlooked the fifteen acre farm, one smaller room she converted into her office, a bathroom with a claw-foot bathtub, and a nice-sized kitchen with an eat-in area. It was perfect for her. Ty hadn't lived with her, but had usually slept over on the weekends, thus the need for the now dearly departed toothbrush.

But now that she had put some distance between them, she had come to realize that Ty wasn't the right man for her, as she had once thought. He wasn't exactly a go-getter; his father had done the go-getting, and Ty had lived the typical life of the privileged son. The private schools, the flashy cars, the Ivy League college, the semester abroad. Ty was spoiled and selfish. And maybe that was their problem. Maybe he just didn't love anyone else as much as he loved himself.

Molly, on the other hand, wasn't poor by any means, but she hadn't had a trust fund waiting for her either. Her parents paid for her college education and provided her with a used Chevrolet Malibu at age sixteen so she could get around town, but her life was far from extravagant. Her one connection to the elite was her horses through hunter jumper competitions and the occasional fox hunts. That was where she had met Ty, in the hunt fields.

The winter sky was bright, and the air was crisp on that late December afternoon more than four years ago. Aboard a striking black Warmblood, Molly spotted Ty immediately but didn't have the nerve to speak to him. It turned out that she didn't have to as he came over later to introduce himself, and that was the beginning. *We did make a beautiful couple*, she thought wistfully, *but there's more to a relationship than looks.*

Both were equally lithe and lean with Molly at five foot eight and Ty at six foot two. Ty with his proverbial tall, dark, and handsome good looks complimented Molly's fair skin, light brown hair, and hazel eyes. Both had chiseled features with high cheek bones and simple, beautiful smiles. But as one year was enveloped into another, their conversations grew shorter and their time apart grew longer.

After she and Ty split, Molly's well-meaning friends thought it best for her to jump right back into the dating scene, claiming the best fix for a broken heart was a warm body in her bed. "The best way to get over someone is to get under someone else," her sister had said.

Yikes, Molly had thought. But not wanting to disappoint, she agreed to each and every date. And though she felt she needed some time alone to heal, she couldn't deny that she was lonely. Her career of choice was a solitary one, so she sometimes craved a little social interaction. But she always returned home remembering why she preferred the company of her horses to any man.

Currently, however, there was no main equine companion in her life. Traveller, her partner-in-crime for all of Molly's teenage years and early twenties, was now in semi-retirement. An easy hack through the woods here and there was all the twenty-five year old Thoroughbred could handle. But Molly still loved him just the same, even if he didn't require the same attention and training demands of his youth. Now he preferred to spend his days grazing in the field, chatting with the other senior citizens of the stable, Erin's twenty-two year old Thoroughbred mare, Ruby, and their mom's eighteen year old Quarter Horse gelding, Patriot. They had all earned their semi-retirements, and Molly was glad her parents' thirty acre farm allowed them the freedom to live out the rest of their days in peace and tranquility.

Molly wanted another horse, something young, a project, but she just hadn't found the time to search for the perfect partner. Maybe that was something she'd do this summer.

Now sitting in her office, Molly gazed at the many books on her shelves and at the horse show ribbons hanging on her walls. When she noticed a few empty spaces on the shelf where pictures of she and Ty had once stood, she let out a hearty sigh. *It's definitely time for a break*, she thought, *a break from my life and everyone in it.*

Having just published her last book, it was the first time in months that Molly wasn't on a strict deadline. She could come and go as she pleased without worrying if she was allowing enough time to write. Thinking a change of scenery was in order, she opened her laptop and pulled up her email. She knew exactly where she'd go, "Back to old Kentucky."

As she waited for her messages to pop up, she thought of the verses of the James Tandy Ellis poem. "I want to get back to the old time hills, Where the corn juice runs from the old distills, I want to get back, yes, the good Lord knows, I want to get back where the Bluegrass grows, Back in old Kentucky." Her best friend, Macy, was currently residing where the bluegrass grows, and Molly knew Macy would be ecstatic to have a visitor for the summer.

Since it was Saturday night, she didn't have too many messages and clicked on the one from Erin first.

Her email was typical – short and sweet.

How did the date go? Is there a brother-in-law in my future? Love you – E.

Molly and Erin were two years apart, and unlike many sisters who are that close in age, they hardly ever fought. Their mother reasoned it was because their personalities were so vastly different. Erin was extremely outgoing, always had an opinion about something, and craved attention. Molly could never fathom Erin's need for the spotlight, so she was content to sit back and watch her sister run the show.

But they made up for their opposite personalities in physical appearance as many people confused them as twins. Erin is a tad shorter at five foot six, but their hair, eyes, and features were practically identical. This never bothered Molly as she had looked up to Erin for as long as she could remember. She remembered watching her ride, and Erin was so daring and confident in the saddle. Molly longed to be like that and rode hard until she was.

In school she loved it when teachers would do a double take on the first day of school and then say, "Oh my – for a second I thought you were your sister!" When Erin's friends, the "cool girls" in Molly's opinion, would walk by, they'd give her a high five, "What's up Erin's lil sis?" There was no one else she'd rather be compared to.

Now Erin lives thirty minutes away in Baltimore City with her husband, Kevin, and is an attorney for a large law firm in the old Legg Mason building in the Inner Harbor. Erin is fierce in the courtroom, just like she was in the show ring and on the cross country course.

It's no surprise then, given their different characteristics and tastes, that Molly is the writer. She prefers to be in the background, observing, telling the story. Let Erin stand front and center. Molly knew they each shined in their own ways.

She replied back to Erin, laughing slightly as she typed.

Haha – no brother-in-law! Not even close! He paid more attention to his phone than he did to me. On a lighter note though, the Chicken Chesapeake was really good – shame the company was so bad. Hope you're having a good night with Kevin. I'm getting ready to email Macy. I think a small vacay to Lexington is in order! Talk to you tomorrow. Love you, Molly.

As she pulled up a blank email and typed in Macy Holland's address, Molly thought about the girl who had been her best friend since second grade. Macy, like her sister, was the outgoing one in the friendship. With her curly blonde hair and bright blue eyes, Macy had always been popular with the boys. But Macy was humble and truly the girl who didn't know she was gorgeous. Instead of being someone's arm candy, Macy had spent all her free time in the stable, riding and competing in dressage, a discipline that required precision and perfection in order to excel.

And Macy did excel. She showed her Warmblood, Hunter, up and down the east coast, bringing home the blue ribbons from Devon and showing on the winter circuit in Wellington, Florida. She got so into it that, after ninth grade, she was home-schooled by her mother so she could make more time for lessons, competitions, and traveling. Secretly, Molly had been jealous of the constant riding and training; it seemed like heaven.

Macy has since retired Hunter and took him with her when she went to vet school in Kentucky. Now, it's only fitting that she's completing her internship at Rood & Riddle Veterinary Hospital in Lexington. Hunter, her ever-faithful companion, is still with her, content to munch on the infamous bluegrass all day and be Macy's trail horse. Many times Macy would exclaim how Hunter had been her "saving grace" during vet school. When she was stressed with exams and clinicals, she always knew Hunter would be her brief respite into a world of peace and serenity. She'd hack out into the fields for an easy ride and escape the pressures of her chosen profession.

With all her friends and family still in Maryland, and with her all-work-and-very-little-play situation, Molly knew Macy would be thrilled to have a visitor.

Molly's fingers flew across the keys as she quickly typed out an email to her friend, anxious to get moving.

Hey Dr. Mace! How have things been? Hunter's well, I hope. I'm going cut to the chase. I'm dying here – I can't take anymore blind dates and could really use a break from Maryland right now. Can I take you up on your offer to come visit? If it's cool with you, I'd like to make it an extended one – maybe most of the summer. I'm finished writing right now and think a change of scenery is exactly what I need after everything that's happened this year. So – when can I come?

Love,
Molly

Ps...I'm assuming you're going to say "Yes, come now," so I'm going to start packing! Love you!

Now that the decision had been made to pick up and go, Molly felt slightly disheartened. *But I'm not running away*, she told herself. *I'm giving myself a much-needed break from my crazy life!*

Simple in nature, Molly didn't have too much to pack; she had always been a less is more kind of person and hated clutter. Some clothes for the warm weather, riding gear, a handful of books, and her laptop – that was really all she'd need for the next six weeks or so. When her computer alerted her to a new email and she saw Macy's immediate response urging her to "hurry up and get here already," Molly knew she had made the right decision.

She would take the next day to run errands and get everything in order, and then she'd pack up and head eight hours west to the Horse Capital of the World.

~ Chapter 2 ~

"Yes, that's it. Harder. Harder!" Screamed Cassidy Winters, as she worked her hips beneath Beau Bridges, her handsome co-worker. She wrapped her legs around his strong torso, positioning herself just right, making the most out of his powerful thrusts. Though she was petite, Cassidy was flexible, and she worked alongside Beau until they both climaxed.

Panting heavily, Beau rolled over and immediately felt remorseful. He had promised himself that the *last* time with Cassidy would be the last. He couldn't believe he let this happen again. Didn't he have any self-control? But he had had a few beers, and Cass had been coming on strong, as usual, and one thing had led to another.

When he looked over at her, she was smiling contentedly. *Boy, what I am getting myself into*, he thought. Sure, Cass had said she didn't want anything serious either – told him that she was cool with being friends with benefits, but he didn't buy it. Not anymore. Her actions at work, like surprising him with coffee exactly how he took it, and that sly look on her face right now, were telling. She wanted more, and he just couldn't give that to her. What they'd been doing for the last three months was wrong, and Beau knew it.

This was it, he thought to himself. *It has to be.* He couldn't keep leading this poor girl on. And even though Cass was a sweetheart with beautiful red hair and a gorgeous smile, his heart just wasn't in it.

"Want some breakfast?" Cassidy asked as she reached over and traced the outline of his six-pack with her finger. "I know it's still dark out, but I've worked up quite an appetite." She smiled playfully, and Beau's heart ached for the pain he knew he would bring to her.

"Honey, I'd love some food, but I've got to get going." He glanced at his watch. "I'm on nightshift tomorrow, so I really need to go home and get some shut eye." Beau could see the hurt in Cassidy's eyes as he declined her offer, but she put on a brave front, her smile barely wavered. "But thanks anyway," he said as he sidled out of bed and quickly dressed. He could feel Cass' eyes rolling over him.

Beau was tall and lean, every bit of six foot four. His arms were long and sinewy yet muscular, and the way he walked commanded attention. His brother called it a "swagger," but Beau wasn't too sure about that. His medium brown hair complimented his dark green eyes, and his chiseled, even features completed the package. An olive complexion made his eyes pop all the more, and Cassidy always wondered how someone whose job kept him inside all day could still be so tanned.

"No problem," she said somewhat easily. She could tell that he was anxious to leave, but she didn't want to let on how much this bothered her. Yes, she had told him that she was fine with some recreational sex, but of course she didn't mean it. Well, she had hoped that that would be enough for her, that she'd take what she could get and just enjoy it. But of course her feelings had gotten in the way as she'd had a major crush on Beau from the moment she started working with him at Rood & Riddle Veterinary Hospital. Every girl at the hospital did. What was not to love about him?

Beau finished dressing and flashed Cass one last smile as he grabbed the keys to his truck. "See you at work," he said, walking out of Cassidy's bedroom and heading for the back door.

Once outside he let out a sigh of relief. He had to end this. Not only was it not fair to toy with Cass on a personal level, she was also a co-worker. That was frowned upon at the hospital, of course, even though everyone knew things went on behind closed doors, especially during night shift. But it wasn't professional behavior.

Beau put the key in the ignition and placed the truck in drive. This wasn't like him. Prior to Cassidy, he had never slept with a girl he worked with. That sort of thing never really interested him – he guessed it made him feel like a cad. And Beau had worked so hard to get where he was in his career that the last thing he wanted was to be distracted at the hospital. *I can't let this happen again*, he thought as he drove home along the deserted Kentucky roads.

~ Chapter 3 ~

So this is how the working world lives, Molly thought as she inched forward at a snail's pace on Interstate-695, Baltimore's beltway. She should have known better than to leave at rush hour.

She had planned to get on the road by five or six o'clock in the morning at the absolute latest, but she had stayed up far too late last night double and triple checking that everything was in order, and as a result, she missed her alarm. *Oh well*, she thought, *what's done is done. It's not like I'm on a strict timeline. I'll get there soon enough.*

After she finally dragged herself out of bed, had her morning coffee, and dressed for the day, Molly chuckled as she surveyed her bags. All of a sudden her spur-of-the-moment trip to escape life had become anything but! The one suitcase she thought she'd need turned into three, not including her laptop, book bag – a bag literally filled to the brim with books – and her riding bag, which contained her helmet, boots, half-chaps, and breeches. *But these are all the essentials*, she laughed to herself. At least her Ford Explorer was large enough to accommodate everything she could not do without during her "Back to Basics Trip," as Macy had started calling it.

Molly recalled the longer email Macy had sent almost immediately after her first one, telling Molly she couldn't wait for her to pack up her car and head west.

Moll – I don't think you realize how great this trip is going to be for you, especially right now. I'm christening it your "Back to Basics Trip," because that's exactly what it is. You're going to come out here and relax, ride, read, and write. You'll have plenty of room here with me – my apartment is the perfect size for two beautiful, single girls in Kentucky! I want you to come and forget about everything and just concentrate on Molly. Got that? I can't wait to see you! Drive safe...but *hurry!*

Love,
Mace

Although Molly was pretty satisfied with her life, especially professionally, she had to admit that she truly wished she could get back to basics. Sometimes she longed to be a carefree, silly eight year old again. No responsibilities, no bills, no hideous boyfriends, just Molly, her parents and sister, and her horses. How simple life had been. What she wouldn't give to get back to that. With a sigh, Molly wondered if the best days of her life were behind her. *No, they can't be – I won't let them be*, she thought, but she couldn't deny the ever-increasing doubts which constantly flooded her mind.

While Molly felt like she didn't have to have a man in her life to make her feel happy, she had to admit that she was lonely. And at age twenty-nine, pickings were getting a bit slim, and she was starting to feel like all the good ones were taken or already married. She thought about Erik, her college boyfriend. Maybe she should have just married him after all. She remembered the first day she and Erik met in the spring semester of their freshman year. They sat next to each other in Statistics, and bonded over their immediate hatred for their snobby, cold-hearted professor, the one who had assigned pages of homework on the very first day of class.

Erik had been her first real boyfriend. He was gentle and kind and had an easiness about him that comforted Molly. She had always felt safe with him, and he was very patient and attentive to her. They dated for almost a year before Molly decided to give him her virginity. Erik had assured her he would take it slow and careful, and he did.

They had been inseparable throughout college and had so much in common, at first. After graduation, he sprung the "good news" on her, and it broke her heart. He had gotten a job on Wall Street in the financial industry. He had assumed that she would follow him, and they would rent a small studio apartment in SoHo or some other trendy section in Manhattan. He'd join the rat race, and she'd stay home and cultivate her craft, having complete freedom to write. And while this offer seemed tempting, and though she loved Erik with everything she had, she knew in her heart that she wouldn't last more than a month as a city dweller. *What about my horses?* No, Erik's news was not particularly "good" in Molly's eyes, and exactly one week later, they broke up.

Erik tore off to New York and climbed his way up the corporate ladder faster than anyone she knew. She had seen on Facebook that he had gotten married last summer, in the Hamptons, to an attorney four years his senior. Molly wished him nothing but love and happiness as she harbored no ill will toward Erik. He had been a wonderful boyfriend, but a future together just wasn't in the cards. Having grown up in downtown Baltimore, he was a city boy with high rise aspirations, and she needed wide open spaces, simplicity, and the sound of crickets at dusk. It broke her heart that he left her behind, that she hadn't been a good enough reason to stay.

I definitely didn't picture myself barefoot and pregnant in my early twenties, but I kind of thought I'd at least be a wife by now, Molly wistfully thought as she drove along the beltway. *But I guess when it's right, I'll know.* Molly laughed as she pictured her mother's sweet face looking up at her and saying, "You know that proverbial ton of bricks, baby? When you meet Mr. Right, they'll hit you, just you wait and see."

When Molly took the exit for Route 70 west, she wondered if this trip was her Manifest Destiny. "Go West, Young Man," had been the motto as the United States began expanding from coast to coast. The mid-nineteenth century had been an interesting time for America, which was still a relatively new nation. Molly liked the idea that by heading west, she too was on the brink of a new beginning.

Almost five hours and one bathroom break later, Molly took a small detour through one of her most favorite towns, Deep Creek Lake. Situated beautifully in the center of Garrett County, the westernmost county in Maryland, Deep Creek had been a frequent family destination for the Sorrensons for as long as Molly could remember.

As she drove along the lake's edge, she couldn't stop herself from reminiscing about the last time she'd come to Deep Creek, this past New Year's, only six months ago. She, Ty, and a large group of their friends always rented a massive ten bedroom house at the very top of the mountain. The view was incredible, and it was the perfect way to ring in the New Year. They'd all pack groceries and wine and unless someone wanted to venture out and ski at the nearby Wisp Resort, there was no need to leave the house. And with multiple levels, games, an indoor pool, and three hot tubs, who would want to?

Molly always packed comfortable clothes and would lounge around all day, reading, writing, and catching up with her friends. She loved being on top of the mountain, loved being able to take in the quiet view of winter. The lake looked so tiny and beautiful from so high up, almost like a painting with crisp edges and clear lines against the shore. She especially loved being there when it snowed, watching the flakes fall silently while inside with a mug of hot tea or coffee clutched tightly against her chest.

Now that she and Ty had split, she figured that was the end to the big New Year's trip. Since most of the friends who came were mutual, it would probably be too awkward to continue. *Another tradition gone – another unwanted change*, Molly sadly thought.

She was making her way down Garrett Highway when Molly decided to make another detour. Year after year Molly's family had rented the same condo and ventured out west to bask in the fall foliage. Though Molly hadn't visited Deep Creek with her family in about three years, she could still picture the condo perfectly, remembering the large stone hearth, the vaulted ceilings, the bookshelf in the hallway piled high with historical non-fiction and mysteries, and the stack of board games behind the couch.

We should take a family trip out here this fall, she thought. *I have so many good memories of this place.* Molly smiled as she made the right turn into the complex. Just after a small wooded area, the condos appeared on her left, the lake just beyond them shone crystal clear in the early afternoon sunlight.

Molly parked just past the small complex, grabbed her cell phone out of her purse, and jumped out of the car. A short jog down the stairs along the bank and she was standing on the pier, watching the scattering of boats glide by on their way to a perfect fishing spot. She took a few pictures and marveled happily that everything seemed exactly the same.

A man and his daughter walked down the pier, spooking Molly who, lost to the past, jumped as they walked by.

"Sorry to scare you," the dad laughed. "Thought you must have heard us with all the racket this one is making." He smiled as he pointed back to his daughter, a brilliant little towhead who couldn't have been more than five years old.

"Oh no, it's fine! I was just in a daze." Molly shook her head to clear it. She looked at the little girl and smiled. "Is your dad taking you out on the boat?" She had on a pint-sized life jacket adorned with Sesame Street characters.

The girl looked at Molly with the brightest green eyes she'd ever seen. She slipped her hand into her father's, but extended her other arm out to show Molly her neon pink fishing rod. "Yep, my daddy's taking me fishing. I even have my own rod!"

"Wow, that's awesome! What a pretty rod! I bet you'll catch all kinds of fish with it." Molly looked back up at the father. "Well, have a nice day. Good luck to you two."

They waved Molly off as she turned and headed back up the hill towards her car. At the top, she sadly turned back to face the lake and wiped a stray tear from her eye. How quickly life can change.

~ Chapter 4 ~

Beau drained the rest of his coffee and then glanced at his watch. It was already three o'clock in the morning, and he'd hardly had time to make his usual rounds. With two emergency deliveries, the more stable horses under his care would have to wait.

Thankfully, both foals had been born with virtually no complications, which was unusual given the difficult labors each mare had endured prior to being shipped to the vet hospital in the middle of the night. The owners of each knew just how lucky they had been. Once a mare drops to the ground and begins to push, the clock starts ticking. If that foal doesn't come out within the next hour, he or she is usually a goner. Upon realizing that their mares were in trouble, both owners loaded their girls on the trailer and sped to the hospital within hours of each other. One had arrived at midnight, the other, just after one.

Beau walked by the stall that housed the first foal born that night, a tiny filly. *What a sweet little face she has*, he thought. Slender and refined, she definitely looked like a girl. Beau always thought it was funny that even animals resembled their gender. The colt next door was on the larger side with boxier features, but he was also going to be a looker.

He gave each mare a pat on the shoulder before he bent down to inspect each baby one last time before rounds. Being broodmares, these old girls knew the drill as neither baby was their first. Both horses allowed Beau to move freely about the stall, instinctively trusting that no harm would come in his care.

Though he loved his job, Beau would be the first to tell anyone just how hard and time-consuming it was being a Doctor of Veterinary Medicine. While explaining his daily responsibilities, he'd unconsciously grab the back of his neck and massage his aching muscles. But he never regretted his decision to take this path in life, though a few obstacles had stood in his way.

Born on a produce farm in Fort Valley, Georgia, Beau learned at a young age how to work hard for a living, working the land from sun up until sun down, cultivating crops and harvesting vegetables. He had seen tragedy in the form of dry, dusty droughts, rainless months that ravaged everything in sight. But working alongside his parents and his older brother and sister, Beau had learned some valuable lessons about life.

Though theirs was a working farm, the Bridges family still had their fair share of fun. On the farm was a large pond for swimming, bordering trails for hiking and exploring, and, most importantly, horses for riding. With his mom's affinity for equines, there were always a number of horses around for pleasure riding, and Beau, taking after his mother, loved every minute he would spend with these exquisite creatures.

By the time Beau was old enough to ride alone, his brother and sister had passed down their fifteen hand Quarter Horse named Dolly. A little on the older side and slightly settled in her ways, Dolly could be as hard-headed as a mule. With her bright bay coat and wide blaze, she was as cute as they came, but Beau's mama always said that she could see the mischief in her eyes. However, Dolly was usually game for anything, and Beau would take her exploring on the trails, galloping across the neighboring fields, and wading in the creek across the dirt road.

He could still remember the exact moment he decided he wanted to be a horse vet; he had been eleven years old. After returning from a particularly long ride, Beau noticed that Dolly had some cuts and scrapes on her lower back legs. He brought her into the barn and put her in the crossties so she'd stand by herself and he could have both hands free.

First, he brought over a bucket of cool water and a sponge. He gently wiped away all the dirt and grim, cleaning the cuts as best he could. Next, he slathered her cuts with an antiseptic cream, and then expertly wrapped both legs. When he stood back to survey his work, Dolly nickered her appreciation and Beau had to admit that he was pretty pleased with his work. Later on he would make sure Dolly received a small dose of bute, an anti-inflammatory and pain reliever, with her evening feed.

Though he was beating himself up for taking Dolly into parts of the trail that had caused these scratches, caring for her afterward had been so satisfying. Even with her stubborn tendencies, Dolly was still a good companion to Beau, and on that day, he had been able to take care of her, for once, and show his gratitude. She was, after all, an excellent little horse.

Beau kept his secret of wanting to be a vet to himself for quite a few years, worried that his parents would be hurt or angry that he had decided against helping with the family farm that they'd had for three generations. And if horses hadn't meant so much to him, he probably would have been content to work alongside his brother and sister, tending to the fields every day. He truly loved this land, but his heart was with horses.

Thankfully, his father saved him the trouble of having to break this news. It was late one evening and Beau was in the barn, as usual, caring for the horses, one by one.

"Hey dad," Beau said when he noticed his father leaning against a stall on the opposite side of the aisle. "I didn't see you there."

"You know, son," he said in that deep, Southern drawl, "I've been watchin' you with these animals for years, and I reckon you're gonna go to school one day to be a horse vet. It just seems fittin'."

Beau remembers being completely taken aback by his father's keen observations, but also excited that he seemed for it.

"Yeah dad, I guess you're right. Horses are my life. There's no place I'd rather be than here with them."

"Alright then, son, I know you'll be great. Make me proud."

And then he turned and was gone. But this was all the encouragement Beau needed, and two years later he was packing up his beat-up Ford and heading north to become a Wildcat at the University of Kentucky. That had been about sixteen years ago.

Working night shift at the hospital could be a little difficult on his sleep schedule, but it was Beau's favorite. He liked the dimness of the hallways and the darkness in the various stalls. He loved watching horses lie down in their beds of straw, snoring softly, deep in sleep. And though it wasn't always quiet, any silence to be had was usually found at night, and Beau would savor it.

As Beau made his rounds, he was joined by Cassidy, who had been serving out her internship with Rood & Riddle for the past six months. Not surprisingly, things with Cassidy had become strained, which was a shame because Beau did enjoy working with her. She asked a lot of questions, and Beau liked her spunk and eagerness to learn. He felt terrible for ruining what should have been a normal working relationship. However, Cassidy did her best to remain professional, and Beau had to give her credit for that.

"I hear you've already had quite the night," smiled Cassidy, who had heard about the two foal deliveries.

Beau smiled back and opened the door to another stall, "Oh yeah, as you know, there's never a dull moment around this place." As he entered, his smile grew even wider. Inside was one of his favorite patients, Gypsy, a two year old Thoroughbred filly. Gypsy was, without a doubt, one of the prettiest horses Beau had ever laid eyes on, and he had seen more than his fair share. With a shiny coat as black as night, a star in the center of her forehead, and a dainty face that could have belonged to an Arabian, Gypsy turned heads.

"There's my special girl," Beau cooed. "How's she doing tonight?" Gypsy, sensing one of her favorite people, immediately turned from her hay net and made her way slowly over to Beau. Both forelegs were wrapped from fetlock to knee in thick bandages, which made walking a challenge. Though she could bend her knees, it was hard to completely flex them, and she gave the appearance of a peg-legged pirate. She was in the hospital suffering from a bowed tendon. It wasn't life-threatening, but definitely career-threatening for her, a future racehorse.

But none of her ailments affected Gypsy's baby doll personality. She sidled up to Beau, draped her head over his shoulder, and exhaled a long, relaxed breath. Beau stood still as Gypsy leaned into him, helping her by supporting some of her weight. He laid his head against her upper neck and stroked her shoulders and withers with his hands.

"You two are quite the pair!" Cassidy laughed. She was always amazed at how the horses responded to Beau. Maybe it was his gentle nature, the way he moved about them, slow and easy, and they all seemed to instinctively know he was a friend and immediately let their guards down in his presence. Cassidy wished she could turn Beau's head the way this filly had.

"She just wants a friend, that's all. Horses need friends, and this one is no exception."

As Beau busied himself in Gypsy's stall, Cassidy let her eyes wash over him. She thought he was the most handsome man she'd met in a long time. Every feature was perfect, but it was Beau's hands that Cassidy liked the best. They were perfectly shaped and manly. As she knew only too well, they could be strong when they needed to be, gentle at other times. Even though they had been together the night before, Cassidy longed for the touch of those calloused hands on her bare skin. She shivered at the thought.

"I'm getting ready to go on break," Cassidy said. "Need anything before I go?"

"Nope, Cass, I think we're good for now," Beau answered as he let himself out of Gypsy's stall. Then he flashed her that easy grin of his and strode back down the hall.

~ Chapter 5 ~

West Virginia is so beautiful, Molly thought as she continued her journey west. She marveled at the scenery as she drove as bend after bend offered the most amazing views. Everything was so bright and green, alive in the mid-June earth. *Summer is without a doubt my most favorite time of the year*, she thought happily to herself.

Before she knew it, evening was upon her, and Molly was crossing the Kentucky state line. She had been to Kentucky once before, but that had been years ago when her sister competed in a three-day event at the Kentucky Horse Park. Molly was probably thirteen or fourteen, but she remembered thinking just how beautiful the area was. She couldn't believe places like this, totally devoted to horses, really existed. She was so excited to be coming back again after all these years.

She started seeing signs for Lexington when she was about an hour west into Kentucky. Molly was getting close and couldn't wait to see her best friend. Macy had received her undergraduate degree at a college back east, but moved out to Kentucky for vet school seven years ago. She had graduated with her Doctor of Veterinary Medicine degree and completed several internships at local equine hospitals. Molly was so proud of her friend. Macy had already accomplished so much in her life and was such an inspiration to those around her, especially given her childhood.

Macy lost her father to cancer when she was only nine years old. His death shook her family to its core, but Macy, her older brother, Tommy, and their mother banded together and got through it. Naturally, those years were very trying for Macy, but she buckled down, persevered with both her riding and her studies, and excelled in each.

Whenever Macy put her mind to something, she gave it her all until she achieved her goal. While Molly was happy that her friend was doing well, she also missed her and hoped that after Macy's final internship was over next year that she would pack up and head home to join one of the local practices, or start her own.

Molly's GPS helped her navigate through the back roads, and she gasped with delight as she drove through some of the prettiest countryside she had ever seen. *No wonder Mace doesn't want to come home,* Molly marveled. *It's gorgeous out here!*

A few minutes later, Molly pulled up to a small apartment complex called Fox Run. Before she could reach for her phone to tell Macy she was here, she saw her friend fling open the front door of her ground floor apartment and come running out to greet her.

"Yay! You made it!" Macy cried. Both girls threw their arms around each other and hugged tightly.

"My goodness Mace, I've missed you so much! You don't know how good it is to see you!"

"I'm so happy you decided to visit! You're going to have the best time. You'll stay the whole summer, and maybe you'll decide not to leave. We'll be roommates forever," Macy giddily mused as she helped unload Molly's things from the car.

It was hard not to catch Macy's infectiously enthusiastic personality. *I definitely made the right decision*, thought Molly. *It feels so good, so comfortable to be with Macy. Maybe there is something to this Back to Basics trip after all.*

"Come in – I've got dinner on the stove. Did I tell you that I've learned to cook? It's actually not that difficult, and when the choices are either learn to cook or starve, you learn pretty quickly." Macy was notorious for her lack of skill in the kitchen, and Molly used to laugh at Macy's standard line, "I can make a pretty mean bowl of cereal!"

"You learned to cook? Look at you, Mace – all grown up! Living the life of a successful career woman and making meals by yourself!" The two girls dissolved into giggles as they made their way into the kitchen for some homemade chicken noodle soup and cornbread.

As they finished their meals and washed their bowls in the sink, they talked about their summer plans.

"So I'm on a rotating shift at the hospital: day, evening, night. I do a week on each, so we'll miss each other a bit every third week when I'm on night shift. Hope you don't mind."

"Not at all! Look, you're doing me a favor by letting me come and crash at your place. Don't feel bad at all. At least you have a *real* job. I'm just a writer."

"Whatever! You're a *successful* author who can actually make a living doing what she loves. Not everyone can say that, you know."

"I know. But your job sounds so great. I'd love to be surrounded by horses all day. Promise me I can come and shadow you sometime. Is that allowed?"

"Sure! I mean, there are some places you can't go, like into surgery, but you can definitely come for mini-tours. You'll love it, Moll, the technology they have these days is amazing. And my colleagues are so nice. There's this one older guy who can be a little pompous, but everyone is truly happy to help and teach."

"Awesome! I can't wait to stop by and meet everyone."

"Come by tomorrow! What are your plans anyway? You know, feel free to go ride Hunter any time you'd like. He could use the exercise and would love to see you."

"I was hoping you'd say that! I'd love to ride such an amazing horse. Can I take him out sometime tomorrow?"

"Of course! And he knows the trails. Just give him his head, and he'll take you on a nice ride. It'll be a great way to see the Kentucky countryside at its finest."

~~~~~

The next day dawned bright and sunny, hot and humid. But being from the East Coast, Molly was used to hazy days that turned her hair into a frizzy mess. She hopped out of bed at seven-thirty, saw that Macy had already left for work, and decided to take advantage of the cooler morning temperature and take a short ride on Hunter. He was stabled at a boarding facility less than ten minutes away from the apartment, and she had no trouble locating the farm.

Some people say that horses are not like dogs, that they don't recognize people from their past, but Molly would have bet against that notion as Hunter came galloping over in response to her high pitched whistle. "Hey boy! So you do remember me, huh? It's so good to see you!"

Hunter looked exactly the same. He was a beautiful chestnut with a striking white blaze that ran down the middle of his face and extended into a wide snip on his nose. *What a good horse you've been*, Molly thought, *truly worth your weight in gold.*

"Can I help you?" Asked a friendly voice behind her.

"Oh yes, hi, my name is Molly. I'm a friend of Macy Holland's. I'm staying with her for the summer, and she said I could take Hunter out occasionally. Is that okay? Do I need to sign a waiver?"

"Oh right, she did mention she had a friend visiting from Maryland. I'm Barb – nice to meet you. Welcome to Fairfield Farm. And yes, I'll need you to sign a waiver. We try and keep things nice and legal around here," she added with a grin. "Come with me. I'll get you all set up and show you where Hunter's tack is stored."

Molly followed Barb back up the long drive to the main barn. The facility was beautiful. There appeared to be two barns, one large one connected to an indoor arena, and one smaller one off in the distance. Both were white and trimmed in dark green. She could see a medium-sized outdoor ring just beyond the main barn, complete with sand or stonedust, she couldn't quite tell, six or seven brightly-colored jumps, as well as dressage letters around the perimeter. *This would be the perfect place to relax after a long, stressful day at the hospital*, Molly thought. *So glad Mace has a place like this in her life.*

After she signed the waiver, releasing the farm from any liability should Molly take a spill and injure herself or Hunter, she followed Barb to the tack room where she located Hunter's things.

"Macy said you are quite the horsewoman, so I guess there's no need for me to hang around and watch you like a hawk!" Barb laughed to herself.

"Nope," Molly laughed. "No need. I've ridden for my entire life, and I'm pretty familiar with Hunter, too. He's like family."

"Well good, have yourself a nice ride. We have some pretty great trails here. Hunter knows where they all are. Just head out back and make a right after the fence-line. That's where they all begin."

"Sounds perfect, thanks for your help."

Hunter was still waiting at the gate when Molly went down to catch him. A big boy at sixteen-three hands, he was just a little taller than what Molly was used to. Traveller is sixteen hands even and a skinny Thoroughbred. Being a Warmblood, Hunter had what her mother liked to say, "a little meat on his bones."

As Molly clipped the crossties onto Hunter's halter and started the pre-ride grooming session, she felt completely at ease. *This is where I belong*, she thought, *out in the barn with horses.* She couldn't wait to get another horse of her own, a young filly or colt that she could start herself. She knew why she hadn't made an active effort to find another horse yet – she felt guilty. Traveller had been the love of her life for many years, and the thought of devoting a lot of time and attention to another horse made her feel bad, like she was turning her back on Trav.

But Molly realized that simply wasn't true. Trav is content being mostly retired, pulled from the field occasionally for a quiet hack around the fields and through the trails. *He wouldn't be jealous*, Molly reasoned. *Besides, I'm just dying to get back to competing. It's been at least five years since I did anything worthwhile in the show ring.*

The trails were better than Molly could have anticipated. Wide and flat, a horse and rider could easily take off at a gallop along these paths under the shady protection of the tree canopy. Most of the trails back home were narrow and hilly – or rocky. Those trails were never ventured through faster than a walk, and a slow, easy one at that.

After Hunter was warmed up, Molly asked him for a nice, easy canter, and he readily obeyed, pushing off with his hind end into that smooth, rocking-horse gait. He was such a well-trained horse that even out in the trails, with no competitors or judges, Hunter was still quite collected and balanced.

Molly had loved watching Macy and Hunter compete together. In their prime, they truly were unstoppable. If she wasn't at a show herself, Molly would tag along and be Macy's groom, holding Hunter when Mace needed a bathroom break, and helping to wrap legs, fix braids, shine boots, and pin numbers to the back of jackets.

Macy could have had a future as a professional on the dressage circuit, but it just wasn't in the cards. "I don't think it would be nearly as fun if it became my work," Macy said. "I don't want winning or losing to mean the difference between being able to pay my mortgage or not. I just don't want that pressure." And Molly completely understood. Horses were family members, not business ventures.

So when Macy decided to pursue vet school, Molly knew that was the right choice. Mace was too good with horses not to work with them every day, but this way she'd have a steady paycheck. And Molly had a feeling Mace would return to the show circuit again.

More so than Molly, competing was in Macy's blood, and she knew Macy couldn't live without it for long. Right now she was content to complete her internship, but as soon as things settled and Macy had a little time on her hands, Molly knew Hunter would get a four-legged brother or sister.

Returning to the barn with a large smile on her face, Molly knew she'd have to make these rides an almost daily occurrence. Hunter seemed to enjoy his time out, and Molly couldn't get enough of this darling horse.

"You're a rockstar, you know that, Hunter? You are such a good boy," Molly cooed after she dismounted and hugged the sweet horse.

Molly went about the post-ride routine of hosing Hunter, picking his hooves, and reapplying fly spray. She gave him an apple, a kiss on the nose, and returned him to his buddies in his field.

When she got back into her car, she saw she had a text message from Macy.

Hey! How was your ride? Was my Hunter a good boy? If you get this while you're still at the farm, come visit me at work. The hospital is only two miles away.

She also included the address and directions.

There's no way I can go out in public looking like this, Molly thought. She was clad in khaki-colored breeches with black paddock boots and half chaps. Her white, sleeveless shirt wasn't too terribly dirty, but she definitely smelled like horse. Her long hair had been pulled back into a simple braid, and as she looked into the rearview mirror, she was delighted to see that she didn't appear too sweaty. *Wait, I'm going to an equine hospital,* she laughed to herself. *I'm sure everyone there smells like horse!* She responded to Macy.

My ride was perfect. Hunter is such a babydoll – missed him so much! I'm just leaving now, will probably be at the hospital in five mins. See you then!

When she pulled up in front of the entrance of Rood & Riddle, she smiled to herself. That Mace is really going places. An internship at one of the top veterinarian hospitals in the country is no easy feat.

Macy, expecting her visitor, walked outside and waved to Molly. The two girls embraced as if they hadn't seen each other in months. One was excited to show off her place of employment to her best friend; the other was high on life thanks to a trail ride exploring unfamiliar territory on a very familiar horse.

"My ride was incredible! I can't believe how great Hunter felt, and his canter is phenomenal. It's like he's never lost his top form," exclaimed Molly.

"That's my boy, a born athlete! So glad you had a great time. And free feel to take him out as often as you'd like. I try and get over there to see him at least every other day, but I usually don't have time to ride more than once a week. He can be your summer horse! And he's perfect for your Back to Basics trip since you two are old friends!"

"You're the best Mace," Molly laughed. "Now show me around. I feel like such a tourist."

Macy took Molly all over the hospital and introduced to her a few of her colleagues, as well as some of her favorite patients, including a sweet filly who was less than twenty-four hours old.

"Her mama was having some complications, so her owners rushed her in here. But both are fine now. Isn't she the cutest thing ever?"

Molly couldn't believe how adorable the little filly was. "She's so soft, and quite social," she laughed as the filly stuck her nose in Molly's face and blew out a sweet breath. "I could take her home with me this instant!"

A few minutes later they were at the stall of an all-black, two year old filly. The horse stuck her head over the stall guard and practically beckoned Molly over to her.

"Oh, isn't this one friendly?" She said as the filly placed her head over Molly's shoulder and wrapped it around her back, giving her a horse hug. "My goodness, she's a doll!"

"That one, she's everyone's favorite," came a voice from the aisle. Molly turned to see a pretty redhead and smiled as Macy introduced the two girls.

"This is Cassidy – we're both interns. Cassidy, this is my best friend, Molly. She's from Maryland and is staying with me for the summer."

"Hi, nice to meet you," said Cassidy as she leaned forward to shake hands. "I apologize for my appearance. I'm dead on my feet. I was on night shift but volunteered to take day shift too because another colleague of ours called out sick. These circles under my eyes are from lack of sleep. I swear, no one punched me!"

"I think you look fine," laughed Molly. "But wow, two long shifts in a row. I don't blame you for being so tired. I don't know how you girls do it, and your work is so physical too."

"Oh you know how it is," said Macy. "You do what you gotta do for your babies," she smiled as she reached up and held the filly close. "And we love caring for our girl, don't we, huh, Gypsy?"

"Gypsy? Is that her name?" Molly asked. "It fits her perfectly."

~ Chapter 6 ~

One more night, thought Beau as he parked his truck in the lot. It was his last night on night shift, and he wouldn't be sorry to see it end. These shifts were always tough on the doctors as they never seemed to get enough sleep to compensate for the time they spent running their legs off during the midnight hours.

With his charts in one hand and a cup of coffee in the other, Beau began his rounds. He prayed tonight would be quiet. It would be nice to slip out into the break room for an hour or two of shut-eye. Tomorrow he would enjoy his day off. His best friend from college, Peter, was in town for work, and they had agreed to meet for a drink before Peter headed back home to Louisville.

He chuckled to himself as he remembered the first day he met Peter. Beau walked into his freshman dorm room and there was Peter, wearing striped tube socks, running shorts, a "Virginia is for Lovers" t-shirt, and the silliest grin Beau had ever seen. Eccentric and boyish, Peter rushed over to shake Beau's hand and declared that they would be friends from that day forward.

What a weirdo, Beau had thought. But sure enough, he and Peter clicked. They liked the same music – country, 80s, and hard rock – and had the same taste in women – tall, sassy, and independent. Beau was a bottom bunk man; Peter wanted the top. Their study habits complemented each other's so neither was in the other's way. Peter quietly burned the midnight oil; Beau silently woke with the chickens. Both were respectful of the other's space and shared a love for animals.

And it was Peter who introduced Beau to Natalie during their sophomore year.

"She's beautiful and smart and so funny. You'll love her," Peter had exclaimed.

"If she's so great, then why don't you date her?" Beau replied.

"You know I'm seeing Angela, and I really like her. I think she may be *the one*."

Beau laughed at this answer because Peter was a hopeless romantic. Every girl was *the one*.

"Besides," hurried Peter, "she's your type. Focused and driven. She has this amazing smile – good teeth, you know – and her hair is long and wavy." When Beau looked unconvinced, Peter added, "and I think it's time you dated a brunette. They're stable."

At this, Beau burst into laughter. Peter was forever making things up.

"Okay, okay – just one drink. I'll meet you at The Barn after my last class tonight. I should get out around nine or nine-thirty."

"Perfect. You won't regret it!" Shouted Peter as he jumped up to head out to his own class. "You can thank me on your wedding day!"

As Beau came out of his reverie, he sighed when he realized that he almost did just that.

~~~~~

It was almost noon by the time Beau finally got into his truck to head home. His shift had ended at seven that morning, but as usual, things that required his attention came up. By the time he had put out several figurative fires, he realized he had forgotten to eat breakfast and was dead tired.

As he drove along the winding country roads in Versailles, Beau thought about Cassidy. He definitely needed to talk to her and clear the air. They were co-workers, and they'd be seeing a lot of each other until her internship ended. He wanted to settle everything now before things got out of hand. Beau owed her that much. He would be honest and upfront and that would be that. Hopefully.

Beau lived in a small house on a large Thoroughbred breeding farm. The house only had one bedroom and had been occupied by the farm's barn manager, but the owners had recently added another house, larger and closer to the barn, so the manager was enjoying the nice upgrade. Beau saw the "For Rent" sign a few years ago when he drove past the farm and immediately inquired.

As he pulled up to his house, Beau sighed deeply and looked around. He was surrounded by so much beauty. The farm was about three hundred acres and was lined with rows and rows of black, four-board fencing. Situated in the middle of this paradise was a large mansion with wide, white columns in the front. It looked like a plantation right out of the Deep South. The owners were in their late fifties and ran an excellent breeding operation. Decisions about their horses' well-being came before any financial ones and these practices had earned the Richardsons and their West Wind Farm an excellent reputation. Beau liked living here, and he knew that the Richardsons enjoyed having a vet on premise.

Once inside his tiny home, Beau kicked off his boots and made his way to his bed. He was getting ready to pull the covers up over his head when his phone rang. It was his mother.

"Hey mama, how are you?"

"Hi honey! I'm doing well – just callin' to check on my youngest baby. I haven't heard from you in a bit."

"Ha – I wouldn't exactly say I'm a baby anymore, but I appreciate you checking in. I'm doing okay. Work's keeping me busy, as usual. Believe it or not, I just got home from my night shift. It required quite a bit of OT today."

"Must have been a wild night. I know you work hard, son, but everyone needs time for play too. I hope you're treatin' yourself right. Found any lady friends?"

"Mama, you sure don't quit, do you? I hate to disappoint because I know how bad you want more grand-babies, but nope, no lady friends. No time to find them. I got a lot of mares that enjoy my company though," he said with a laugh.

"Oh Beau – you and your horses! I'm sure the mares do love you, honey, but mares won't give me grand-babies! You're almost thirty-five now – you can't be wastin' anymore time. I know things haven't been easy for you in the past, but that's over now. Time to move on."

"I agree, mama, I agree. I'm gonna start looking."

"I know you are, son. Now I'll let you get some rest. Just wanted to check in. I love you, sweetheart."

"Love you too mama – bye for now."

When Beau hung up, he couldn't help but smile. He loved and missed his family so much – his mama especially. *Maybe it's time I pack up my practice and head home, set up shop there*, he thought. *After all, everyone still lives a stone's throw from the old homestead. I know they'd love to have me back.*

Beau had been in Kentucky since he was eighteen years old and had loved every minute of it. But recently he had been considering striking out on his own and starting his own veterinary practice. He'd make farm calls and work his own schedule. Maybe he'd bring on an associate or two to help him out. It was definitely something to think about.

He set his alarm clock to wake him up in a few hours so he could meet Peter, rolled over, and was asleep within seconds.

~~~~~

Peter was sitting at the bar located in the back of The Merrick Inn watching a game on one of the various televisions when Beau walked in.

"Hey man, so good to see you!" Peter said as he gave Beau his goofy smile.

"You too, thanks for calling!" Beau was so happy to see his old friend. It had been probably close to a year since they'd last seen each other. After college, Peter briefly returned home to Alexandria, Virginia, but then fled back to Kentucky to reunite with Angela, the college girlfriend who really was *the one*. They married shortly thereafter.

When Peter had asked him to be his best man, Beau couldn't have been prouder. He had grown to love Angela as well and couldn't imagine a better woman to stand alongside his best friend.

They had settled just outside of Louisville, Angela's hometown, and had three rambunctious boys: Peter Jr., Jordan, and Barrett. Beau hadn't seen them in quite some time. Maybe it was time to take more than a day off of work and head up the road for an extended visit.

After they had drank two beers and consumed a large plate of cheese fries, Peter cleared his throat and looked uncomfortable. "Hey, so how are you doing, you know, since Nat? I honestly couldn't believe when I heard. I thought to myself, not you two. Not Beau and Nat. If you guys couldn't make it, how were the rest of us bozos supposed to."

"Yeah, I still can't quite believe it myself. But I guess I'm doin' fine…I mean, what else am I supposed to do, you know? I'll get myself together one of these days. In the meantime, I can bury myself in my work. There are always horses in need of some sort of medical attention."

"I'm sure. It's a good thing you have such a demanding job, keeps your mind off what happened. Do you think it will be like last time? Will you guys get back together again?"

"Nope. We've come to the end of our rope, no question about it. She made it quite clear. And I couldn't go through all this again even if she did return."

"I don't blame you. No one should have to live like that, wondering if their significant other is going to up and take off all of a sudden. But you'll find someone else when the time is right. Have you met anyone?"

"Not really. Haven't been lookin', quite honestly. Mama's been after me to start though – wants more grandkids, I reckon. So I've got to dust off my datin' boots sometime soon or she'll have my head."

"Ah Mama Bridges, love that woman. Give her my best, will ya?" Peter grinned.

"I certainly will. And don't be a stranger 'round here, you got that? I miss ya bud." Beau slapped Peter on the back and ordered one more round.

~~~~~

Beau's walk down memory lane with Peter left him unable to fall asleep that night. Too many memories of Natalie filled his mind, memories of finals study breaks together in his dorm, long walks out by the lake, and planes taking off, leaving him behind. So many years. He had spent so many years loving that woman, but now it was really time to let her go. Clearly she had no problem letting him go.

After tossing and turning for an hour or two, he got up and went into the living room to read for a bit. The newest Journal of Equine Veterinary Science had just arrived, so now was as good a time as any to see what the latest and greatest advances were.

He loved equine medicine. There was nothing better than looking into the eyes of a horse and seeing its soul. He loved their mystery, their mystique. They were puzzles and there was nothing he enjoyed more than trying to figure out what made them tick. A horse is a simple creature, yet humans have made them so complex. *Just like a woman*, he laughed to himself.

Beau honestly didn't know where he'd be in life if he didn't have horses. They have given him everything since as long as he could remember. As a boy, he couldn't wait to jump off the school bus at the end of the day and race to the barn to see Dolly. In high school, in addition to helping his parents on their farm, he would also work for his neighbor, Mr. Andrews, who owned a small horse farm. Beau mucked stalls and provided general horse care to Mr. Andrews' handful of barrel racers.

There was nothing better than the smell of a barn: molasses, alfalfa, and leather.

Beau paged through the Journal for another hour before he fell asleep, the book open across his chest. All night he dreamt of Natalie. She was standing on the other side of a wide, empty field, and she had her hands cupped around her mouth, yelling to him, but he couldn't hear what she was saying. Over and over again he shouted, "What? I can't hear you!" He wanted to go to her, but his feet felt like they were glued down, and he couldn't move.

Finally, Natalie gave up. She stood there for a moment, looking lost and lonely, and then turned and walked away.

~ Chapter 7 ~

As Molly drove home from the grocery store in the late afternoon, she marveled at the scenery stretched out before her. One gigantic horse farm after another lined the winding roads of Frankfort Pike and Georgetown Road. She simply could not get over their magnificence, their sheer grandeur. There were very few horse farms back in Maryland that could compete with these. Maybe Sagamore Farm and Marathon Farm, and probably a few others she didn't know about, but that was basically it. Some of these farms were so large that she couldn't see any structures from the road, no houses, no barns, the properties were just that vast. All she could see were posh, gated entrances. Some had tall stone columns wrapped heavily in ivy while some had shiny gold emblems in the middle of sealed gates with initials emblazoned in the center. *Lexington is where the extravagant come to play,* Molly thought, a wistful smile etched across her face.

When she walked into the apartment, she saw a note from Macy.

Today's my first day of evening shift – 3 to 11. Sorry I won't be around for dinner. Go ride – the heat wave has finally broken!

Molly loved her best friend's one track mind: horses. But the heat wave did break last night, so today dawned cooler with low humidity, perfect for an evening ride. So far, Kentucky summers were just like those back home in Maryland: hazy, hot, and humid. During this type of weather, it was best to ride early in the morning or late at night. Today was one of those rarities.

After she put away her newly purchased groceries, she changed into her riding gear, a light blue tank top and tan-colored breeches. She'd slip into her boots and half chaps at the barn. When she looked into the mirror to tie her hair back, she noticed that it had gotten longer and a little lighter. It reached to almost the middle of her back and now contained a few golden blonde strands. *Ahh summer – you do wonders for the soul*, she thought.

When she arrived at the barn, she was surprised to find it vacant. Usually Barb was around mucking stalls or grooming horses, but Molly didn't see her or any of the other boarders. *How could someone not want to ride on a day like today?* She wondered.

Regardless, Molly enjoyed having the place to herself and hummed quietly as she laced her boots, zipped her half chaps, and tacked up the sweet-mannered Hunter. Today she would take the longer trail off to the right side of the property. Macy had told her that the trail was just as picturesque and peaceful, but would be about an hour or more roundtrip. Molly couldn't think of a better place to be on a day like this.

She warmed up Hunter by trotting him along the fence-line that led to the back of the farm. A silly dappled grey filly in one of the pastures ran up beside them, whinnied, and bucked three times in a row before she raced back to her herd. Hunter, the dependable gentleman, hardly glanced at her, but Molly couldn't help laughing at the filly's antics. *How could anyone not love horses?*

The trail was wide and flat, so Molly squeezed with her legs and asked Hunter for an easy canter, which he transitioned into nicely. She cantered in two-point position, her favorite, as it always made her feel like she was flying, especially if she was cantering up a hill. The sun splashed on her face intermittently through the trees above, and she wanted to close her eyes and live in this moment forever.

When she came to the fork in the trail, she went to the right, eager to see what this new path held. She let Hunter walk along leisurely as she daydreamed about other trail rides back home with her mom and sister.

While her mom wasn't an avid competitor like Molly and Erin, she, too, loved horses more than anything. She was mostly a pleasure rider and had been the best show mom. Caring, supportive, and incredibly knowledgeable about horses, Molly knew how lucky she was to have a mother like hers.

Lost in her daydream, Molly found that the trail ended at large open field. She must have missed a turn as she was sure Macy said it was one large uninterrupted circle within the woods. *Or did it connect over on the other side of this pasture?* She wondered. She knew that the owners of all these farms had thousands of acres and granted the riders free rein on their trails, but she wasn't sure if she was still on Fairfield's property or not.

She looked at her watch; they had only been riding for just over a half hour, so Molly thought they had some extra time to explore. She urged Hunter on with her legs, and into the lush, green field he strode.

The silence, the tranquility, Kentucky was perfect. That saying, "Heaven must be a Kentucky kind of place," is so fitting.

Molly had hoped to find the mouth to another trail through the trees on the other side of the field, but she didn't. She continued on down the side of the field until she caught sight of another fence-line. This definitely wasn't part of the boarding farm's property.

She had just turned around to retrace her steps when she heard a horse whinny behind her. When she turned, she saw a man riding a large Paint horse, and they were trotting toward her. He waved as they drew closer, and then sidled up alongside her and smiled.

"You must either be Macy's friend, or you've stolen Hunter," he laughed. He was long and lean and looked more natural on a horse than anyone she'd ever seen. He was riding western and was wearing a green John Deere cap to keep the sun out of his eyes.

"Uh…excuse me?" Molly stammered, caught off guard by the recognition from this perfect stranger.

He threw his head back and laughed. "Guess that may have come as quite a shock. My name is Beau. I work with Macy at the hospital. She told me last week that a friend was coming to town, and, of course, I know Hunter. Mace and I occasionally get together for a trail ride after a long shift. I rent a house on this farm," he said as he gestured to the fences and barns that had just come into view.

Molly grinned. "Yes, I have to admit that you gave me quite a start! But this all makes sense now. My name's Molly, by the way. I arrived last week."

"Welcome. Ever been to Kentucky before?" He asked.

"Once. My sister competed her mare at the Kentucky Horse Park, but that was about fifteen years ago. I had forgotten how beautiful it is out here. I think I could stay forever."

"Well Macy would certainly like that. She's been going on and on about her friend from Maryland. I reckon she's a little lonely out here with her family back east."

"She is. And I'm such a terrible friend. I should have come out to visit sooner."

"The important thing is that you're here now. How long are you planning on staying?"

"I'm not sure, but probably at least through the end of July. But I guess I'll leave when Mace kicks me out," she laughed.

Beau laughed too, "She would never do that. Say, we're not far from my house. Want to come on up for a cold drink? We can tether Hunter outside, or even untack him and put him in a paddock." Beau asked with a hopeful look in his eye.

Molly paused for the briefest second while she considered this man's invitation. "I'd love to, but I really should head back. Thanks though. Maybe some other time?"

"You can count on it."

Molly figured it was too late to try and find the trail she was after, so she let Hunter have his head, and they strolled home at a relaxing pace. She was still shocked that she had run into Beau. *What are the odds?*

But Beau seemed like a really nice guy, and Molly was surprised that Macy hadn't mentioned him before. Or maybe she had at some point, and Molly had forgotten. Regardless, Molly had been very tempted to take him up on his invitation for a drink. But she was in Kentucky trying to simplify her life, not complicate it by bringing another man into the mix. She probably would have enjoyed talking with him though, especially since Beau is, as her sister would say, "All kinds of handsome." *That he definitely is.*

~ Chapter 8 ~

What was he thinking, asking her back for a drink? Where had that come from? Except for whatever Beau had with Cassidy, he hadn't made any sort of move with a woman in, well, too long to remember. And he had been real disappointed when she said no. What could that mean? Beau knew he wasn't ready to date, knew he wasn't ready to test the waters yet. Hell, if he were, wouldn't Cassidy be the perfect woman to start with?

No, he wasn't ready, even if his gut did do a flip-flop over Molly. Besides, Macy said Molly had escaped to Kentucky to get a break from reality, and that she was nursing a broken heart. Maybe it was best to just leave her alone, let her work through her grief without any distractions.

But those eyes, and her smile. She was stunning – absolutely beautiful. She was friendly, but had a quiet self-assurance that he liked. He could tell that she was comfortable in her own skin. He liked that.

Maybe he'd just inquire about her a little. He'd tell Mace that he ran into Molly and just put some feelers out. See if her best friend thought Molly would be ready for a simple date.

Hell. What on earth am I doing?

All Beau knew was that he wanted to see her again. He wanted to see that bright smile again. And maybe he wouldn't call it a date, just dinner or even coffee one night. What's the harm in getting to know a new friend?

But he sure did like the look of this new friend. He liked the way her golden brown hair was braided neatly into a ponytail. He liked the sound of her voice, the ease of it. And he liked the way she sat on a horse. Macy had told him that Molly was quite the equestrian, so already there was some common ground.

Yeah, he'd talked to Mace tomorrow. See what she thought.

~~~~~

"So I hear you scared the crap out of my friend." Macy's voice giggled behind him. "She said, 'and here's this total stranger asking about you and Hunter. I was like, are we wearing name tags or something?'" Macy dissolved into laughter.

"Yeah, her face was pretty funny. I didn't mean to shock her, but I was just surprised to see her. You had just been talking about her the other day and how she was taking Hunter out regularly. She seems like a real sweet girl."

"Yep, she's pretty cool," she said with a sly smile. "You liked her, didn't you?" He had to give it to Macy, she never minced words.

Beau grinned and looked at the ground. "Yeah, she's a pretty little thing. But she's out here gettin' over someone, right?" May as well just come right out with it.

"Well, kinda. She and her ex have been broken up for a few months, so I'd say she's mostly over him. She's really just getting away from all her well-meaning friends and family who keep setting her up on blind dates."

"So she probably wants to be left alone."

"Oh I don't know about that. It never hurts to ask." Macy smiled coyly and walked away.

~~~~~~

Gypsy was showing signs of only gradual improvement. Her ultrasounds looked a little better, but she was still moving around stiff-legged even after Beau had replaced her bulky bandages with a sleeker set. Beau had seen much more severely bowed tendons before, but if Gypsy was ever going to be a racehorse, she'd have to make some major progress, and fast.

Beau ran his hands down her legs, checking for any signs of heat or swelling. The filly bent her head over and blew a sweet, hot breath into his ear, tickling him with her whiskers and making him laugh. He stood and took a hold of her muzzle, looked at her delicate face. "You're something else, you know that? Your legs may not be the best, but your personality is one of a kind."

He lingered in her stall for a few more minutes, tousling her mane and scratching behind her ears. She leaned into his caresses, desperate for affection. He sure was falling for this girl. He just hoped he could get her back on her feet and back into training. Her owners were already starting to pressure him for a good diagnosis.

Back out into the hall, he grabbed the rest of his charts and went in to look at his next patient. In his box stall stood Cash, a four year old Appendix Quarter Horse gelding with chronic uveitis, a condition in which horses develop recurring ulcers in the eye. Cash was plagued with one ulcer after another, and with his beaming light, Beau could see a large, round, ashen-colored ulcer located in the dead center of the eye. In order to detect its true size, however, Beau had to stain the eye, which meant injecting a greenish dye into the eye. This stain adhered directly to the ulcer and in a special light the ulcer glowed as bright as day.

Cash had been getting tube after tube of medication slathered in his eye three to four times a day, but the eye hadn't shown much improvement. While Beau didn't think Cash would lose his sight, he was glad his owner was proactive and brought him in for a Subpalpebral-Lavage-System, a minimally invasive procedure that did require some supervision.

With this procedure, a tiny catheter was inserted through and stitched into the top of Cash's eyelid, making it easy for Beau to administer virtually constant medication directly to the affected area. While the catheter was in place, Cash would need to be kept in the hospital and attended to in order to make sure the device stayed in place. Once he showed some improvement, Beau would remove the catheter and send his patient home.

Cash was a handsome liver chestnut with chrome – a large star on his forehead with four white socks on his legs. His owner had him in training as an eventer and was determined to stay on top of his issue. Beau loved working with owners like this, owners who viewed their horses as pets, as family, not as investments. But he understood that this was Lexington, Kentucky, and horseracing was the locals' business of choice. If the horses didn't earn their keeps, the mortgage wasn't paid. Beau got it. But he didn't particularly like it.

As he finished up with Cash, he started to think about Molly and mulled over a few different ideas. His gut instinct said to leave her alone. She was out in Kentucky getting over a break up, and he was fairly sure that Natalie still had a hold of some of his heart.

But he was never going to get back together with Natalie, and he knew it. *Isn't it time I finally moved on*? Beau thought to himself. *And Molly is so beautiful.*

~ Chapter 9 ~

The next day dawned hot and sticky. The brief cool reprieve Lexington had from the mid-June heat was over. Still, forever outdoorsy girls, Molly and Macy sat outside on the small, shaded patio drinking lemonade and chatting before Macy had to head off to work. They had just finished a lunch of grilled cheese sandwiches and fresh strawberries sprinkled with sugar.

"Ah," said Macy as she stretched her arms back over her head and slouched in her chair. "You're never too old for a grilled cheese sandwich, that's what I always say."

Molly giggled. "Agreed," she said emphatically. "But the fruit made it seem more grown up, didn't it? I guess we're adults after all."

Macy looked over at her friend and smiled. "I really am so happy you're here. This is going to be the best summer, and hey," she grinned devilishly, "you even have a love interest! There's nothing better than a summer fling."

"Oh no I don't," Molly replied. "Beau seemed nice, but I doubt he'd seriously be interested in me. Besides, I didn't come to Kentucky hoping to find a husband. I came to get a break from men, remember?"

"I know, but he is really nice; all the girls at the hospital are crazy about him. You don't need a break from men in general, just the stupid ones you've met on blind dates. And Beau definitely is not stupid."

"Then why haven't you gone out with him?" Molly inquired.

Macy thought for a moment. "I don't know. Call me crazy, but I just don't see him like that. I've always

57

viewed him as my mentor first, friend second. And actually, he reminds me a lot of Tommy," Mace laughed, "and I could never date anyone who looks like my brother!"

Molly laughed too. Now that Macy had brought it to her attention, Beau did resemble Tommy, Macy's older brother.

"You're right. I can definitely see that!"

"And honestly, I don't think I could date someone I work with. My future husband will love horses, of course, but he won't be a vet or even work in the industry. He'll be something all his own. I would hate to compete against my own husband and show him up on a daily basis," Macy winked.

"That makes sense. You'll find someone who's both supportive of what you do but has his own life. But he must love Hunter. That's a must."

"Oh yes," said Macy. "If Hunter doesn't approve then I'll kick that man to the curb," she laughed. "But just so you know, Hunter *does* approve of Beau and likes him very much. And if I remember correctly, didn't you used to have a crush on Tommy? Why not date his Kentucky twin?" Macy was really on a roll.

"You are impossible," Molly cried as she fake-swatted at her best friend. "But yes, I did have a crush on Tommy – who didn't?" Macy's brother was three years older and gorgeous. Too bad he ended up marrying his high school sweetheart. No one else ever had a chance.

"So I can give Beau your number then?"

"Oh you!" Molly looked at her friend exasperatedly. "Yes. Fine. But don't make me look desperate!"

"Oh honey," Macy said. "You couldn't look desperate if you tried."

~~~~~

To her surprise, Beau called later that night and asked her to dinner the following day. Their conversation had been short and sweet as Beau was in between seeing patients. She found it touching that he had wasted no time, squeezing in the call during his work day, no less.

Knowing she was new to the area, Beau thought he'd pick her up early and drive southeast to the small, sleepy town of Berea. They'd browse some of the artisan shops along South Main Street and then have dinner at The Boone Tavern. Molly had never been to Berea, but Mace assured her that it was adorable, and that she'd absolutely love it.

Beau was picking her up at two o'clock that afternoon, and with only two hours to go, Molly realized that not only did she not have anything to wear, but that she was also nervous.

She hadn't packed too many nice clothes for her Back to Basics trip, nothing that she'd wear on a date. Her suitcase had been crammed with shorts and tank tops, breeches and socks. There were no dresses or skirts, no blouses or fancy sandals. And no time to go shopping.

Thankfully, she and Macy were about the same size. Molly was two inches taller, but they both had narrow frames and small waists. Into Macy's closet Molly went in search of something that Beau would find enticing. The last thing she thought she'd be doing in Lexington is going on a date, but Molly had to admit to herself that she was, while nervous, excited too. There

was something different about Beau, and she was
intrigued.

She had enjoyed her encounter with him on the
trails. He had a pleasant demeanor, but came across as
strong and confident. And Macy had nothing but
wonderful things to say about his work at the hospital. He
was intelligent, quick-witted, and humble, she had said.

After trying on a few skirts that were a tad too
short, showing a little more leg than she'd like, she
settled on a blue and white striped sundress. She
borrowed Mace's brown strappy sandals as well, and
with some earrings and a silver bracelet, her look was
complete.

Molly twirled around in front of the full length
mirror in Macy's room. She looked very preppy. *Perfect*,
Molly thought. *I am from the east coast after all.* And she
loved the dress. The straps over her shoulders made her
feel secure, and while it hugged her curves, it wasn't
tight. The hem fell a few inches above her knees – just
right.

Blessed with naturally straight hair, Molly knew
she wouldn't have time to add a million little curls.
Instead, she ran her flat iron down her locks until they fell
well past her shoulders, long and shiny. A little eyeliner,
bronzer, and lip gloss, and she was ready to go.

~~~~~

Beau knocked on the door at two o'clock sharp
and escorted Molly to his Ford F150. As he opened the
door for her to climb into the passenger side, he
complimented her. "Molly, you sure do look amazing.

Those blue stripes really make your eyes shine." Molly blushed a little as she mumbled a thank you.

"Macy said Berea is adorable," Molly said once they were on the road. "I'm really looking forward to seeing the little town."

Beau smiled from the driver's seat. "It is really nice, but they roll up the sidewalks at five o'clock. If we want to browse through any of the shops, we need to get there early."

On the forty minute drive to Berea, Beau talked about his job and how blessed he felt to go to work every day doing something he loved. He told her about some of his co-workers, and that he especially liked working with Macy. "She's a silly one, that's for sure. But she has a great head on her shoulders, and the horses love her."

"That sounds like my Mace, silly and smart. Sometimes I get so jealous thinking about her living out here in The Horse Capital of the World, working alongside brilliant people like you."

"Oh I wouldn't go that far," Beau beamed. "And Macy says you're an excellent writer."

"That's sweet of her. I guess I'm okay as I can afford to make a living off of my writing. I don't make a lot by any means, but my lifestyle is far from extravagant. But writing is so isolating, you know? It's just me and my computer in the little carriage house I rent back home. It's definitely a little lonely, but I wouldn't change it. I couldn't imagine doing anything else."

"That's all that matters," Beau glanced at her and smiled. "You're happy in your work. That goes a long way. Very few people can honestly say that."

As they drove down South Main Street of quaint Berea, Molly couldn't take her eyes off the cute shops and restaurants. After they parked, they strolled through some of the stores, and Molly was amazed at how serene the entire area felt.

"Believe it or not," Beau informed her, "this is a college town. Berea College is just down the street. The school promotes the understanding of service and labor, and each student is required to take a job within the community in addition to their studies. It becomes part of their academic program."

"What a great idea. I wish I had known about this place when I was looking at colleges. I love it here."

In another shop, Molly was especially impressed with the amount of items that had been handcrafted by local artisans. She squealed when she saw a stuffed fox dressed in a hunting habit. With a black helmet, red jacket, and black knee boots, he was quite stunning. "I can't believe someone made him; I've got to get him for my mom. He'd go perfectly in her library."

The Boone Tavern was located in the heart of the town, so at five o'clock they made their way to the restaurant.

The Boone Tavern is more than just a restaurant – it's an Inn with numerous rooms and suites and also boasts a small gift shop. The décor on the inside is sophisticated country, plain and simple, with a blue and white motif throughout that complement the large, white plantation-esque columns outside.

After Molly and Beau were seated and their drink orders had been taken, the waiter returned with a pan of spoonbread fresh out of the oven. Spoonbread is a moist cornmeal-based dish that can be cut, similar to cornbread. It's served hot and with a little butter, salt and pepper, it's a perfect treat.

Molly had never had spoonbread before, but after one bite, she was hooked. She made a mental note to stop at the gift shop on the way out and pick up a pre-made ingredient pouch of it to make for Macy.

Over appetizers of fried green tomatoes, Molly told Beau a little about herself. She had never left Maryland, not even for college. She had attended the local high school, Hereford High, one of the largest in Baltimore County, and then Goucher College, a small liberal arts school, also local, in Towson. Goucher was located about twenty minutes south of her parents' farm, and she had majored in Creative Writing and double minored in English Language and Literature and American History.

"I actually enjoyed being a commuter. My sister used to tell me that I missed out on the *real* college experience by not going away, but I just never had any desire to. I wanted to stay home with my horse, continue to compete, and be with my family. My parents and I have a wonderful relationship. I just didn't see the need to get away."

"Where did your sister go for college?"

"She went to the University of Maryland – it's a massive school, a little city, essentially. She majored in Business Administration, and then got her Law degree from there as well. I enjoyed visiting her and cheering on the Terps, their basketball team, but I was always glad to leave. It felt so claustrophobic with all those people crowded around. I need space."

With that, Beau smiled. He and Molly had a lot in common.

Molly surveyed her surroundings and smiled. "I think this is one of the best restaurants I've ever been to, and I haven't even had my entrée yet," Molly exclaimed. "The spoonbread was to die for, and the fried green tomatoes are amazing. They're not as good as my grandmother's, but they're a close second." She paused and looked at him with a twinkle in her eye. "Can I have the last one?" She asked, grinning like a Cheshire cat.

Beau laughed. "Of course, please help yourself."

Their entrees did not disappoint. Molly enjoyed a meal of roasted chicken, while Beau tucked into his roast beef and baked potato. Molly was amazed at how easy it was to talk to Beau. He was a good listener, quietly offering his thoughts at the right time. She felt like she had known him forever.

Beau, too, was feeling the same way. Rarely did he feel this relaxed with a woman as beautiful as Molly. She was much less shy than she had been that day in the woods, and he told her about life back in Georgia.

"It was a great place to grow up, and sometimes I think about moving back home and starting my own practice. The experience I get at Rood & Riddle is unmatched though. Some of the cases that come in would blow your mind, and, of course, our technology is top of the line. I don't think I'll leave any time soon, but maybe someday." He smiled, "My mama keeps pushing for it, at least."

"Are you very close to your family?"

"Oh yeah. Mama and I talk every couple of days, and I'll give my brother and sister a ring about once a week. My dad usually jumps on the phone when I'm talking with mama, and even though he's a man of few words, you always know where you stand with him."

"So everyone is still local to Fort Valley? Do they all work on the farm?"

"Yep, everyone's local except for me, a fact that mama likes to remind me of pretty regularly," Beau joked. "But I always knew that working a produce farm wasn't for me. I enjoy hard work and being outside, but I could never stay away from the horses. Sometimes I feel guilty that I've been away from home for so long, especially with dad's heart attack and all last year, but he has my mama, brother, sister, and their spouses to look after him. And he's doing pretty well now, even though mama likes to tell him he's still on light duty."

"Your family sounds great, very supportive and loving."

"They really are, and I miss them a lot. But, luckily, my work here keeps me pretty busy, so I'm not too lonely." He then told Molly about some of his current patients at the hospital. When he mentioned Gypsy, Molly's eyes lit up.

"Wait – is this the black filly with the in-your-pocket personality?" Beau nodded. "I met her last week, and she absolutely stole my heart. Will she ever race again?"

"Well, she's actually never raced, was just in training. But the bowed tendon has had her out of commission for a while, and it's not looking good. I'd like some more time to evaluate her, but I'm starting to think that her racing career is over before it started."

"Oh that's a shame," Molly said. "What will happen to her?"

"Her owner will find her another home, I'm sure. With some time off, she'd definitely be fine for another career, hunters, dressage, or what have you, so they'll probably try and place her quickly. Unfortunately, racing is a business, and if the horses aren't winning and making money, then they've got to go."

Molly sighed. "I could never look at a horse as a business investment. They're family."

Beau nodded. "I couldn't agree more, but that's just how things are around here. Thankfully, there are a lot of rescues and placement organizations that specialize in off-the-track Thoroughbreds. And Gypsy is a looker and a sweetheart. She won't have any trouble finding a home."

Molly looked at Beau inquisitively but was silent. Her eyes then took on a faraway look, and the wheels in her head were turning.

~~~~~

Dinner had been absolutely delicious, and both Beau and Molly were stuffed. They shook their heads sadly when the waiter asked if they would be having dessert. They both agreed that the chocolate bread pudding sounded simply mouth-watering, but neither could do it. When Beau suggested they come back another time for the pudding, Molly sincerely hoped that they'd get the chance to do so.

On the way out, Molly bought three pouches of spoonbread, promising to make them for Macy. Then they headed back to Beau's truck and started for Lexington.

When Beau asked her if she'd like to come back to his place for a nightcap, she readily accepted. She wasn't ready for this evening to end. It was so nice to spend time with someone like Beau. *How is it possible for two people from such different backgrounds to be so similar?* Molly wondered.

As he mentioned to her that day in woods, Beau rented a small house on a large breeding farm. When Molly walked in, she noticed that it was furnished like a typical bachelor pad but with an equestrian flair. The walls were mostly bare and the furniture was sparse, but there were equine medical journals scattered about on the coffee and end tables, and an old western saddle sat on a rack in the corner. The leather was worn and cracked, and while it had been oiled recently, Molly thought the saddle was definitely enjoying its retirement.

Beau followed her gaze. "That was my favorite saddle as a kid. It fit my horse, Dolly, like a glove. That mare was my best friend." He pointed to a picture on the mantle where she saw a small boy with rosy cheeks and brown hair smiling brightly as he sat astride a bay horse. He was wearing a cowboy hat that was a little too big for him and a silver belt buckle that dwarfed his tiny waist.

"How cute," Molly said. "Such a sweet picture, a beautiful memory. I have similar pictures with my pony, Sundance. Childhood horses are angels sent from Heaven, aren't they? They have so much to teach."

When Beau didn't answer, Molly turned around to see if he was still in the room, and he was. He was staring at her with a contented look in his eye. "Sorry," he whispered. "I'm listening. I was just thinking how happy I am to have met you. You and I," he said, taking a few steps closer to her, "are a lot alike."

Speechless by this sudden display of emotion from such a rugged man, Molly just stood there and nodded. Beau crossed the room and stood right in front of her. He took her face in his hands and smiled down at her. "I'm so glad you got lost in the woods last week."

"Me too," she whispered.

And with that, Beau leaned down to kiss her, gentle and soft. He continued to cradle her face in his hands and caressed her smooth cheek. Molly leaned into him and wrapped her arms around him, fingers crawling up his muscular back. She hadn't been kissed like this in months. Certainly Ty hadn't held her this way in ages. The last year of their relationship had been very perfunctory.

A slight moan escaped Molly's lips, and Beau had to force himself to pull away. If they didn't part now, he wasn't sure they ever would. As much as it pained him, he lifted his head and opened his eyes. Molly stared up at him looking like an angel, innocent and sweet.

~ Chapter 10 ~

"So I heard you went on a date last night. I want to hear all about it," Molly's mom, Karen, said matter-of-factly. Molly and her mom spoke almost every day, but she could tell this day's conversation was going to be a little different.

"Who told you I had a date?" Molly asked, incredulously.

"Macy texted Erin, and Erin told me. So I hear he's a vet, huh? Good girl Molly – we could use one of those in the family." Molly could hear the smile in her mother's voice.

"Oh mom, you are too much, and yes, he's a vet. He and Macy work together, but I actually met him while I was out with Hunter on a trail ride. It was just a total coincidence."

"And what's this young man like? When will I get to meet him?"

"Mom! I don't know – maybe never! I just met the guy," Molly exclaimed. Sadly, she knew her mom was only half joking.

She spent the next half hour answering her mom's many questions about Beau and their date. Karen was intrigued to learn that he was from Georgia and had left his entire family, and their business, behind to become a horse vet. She admired his determination to follow his passion, even if it meant striking out on his own.

"Well he sounds perfect for you: kind, intelligent, and, of course, an animal lover. But does he like books?" Karen laughed. She knew her daughter so well and knew her two greatest loves in life were horses and books.

"I'm not sure, but I did see a bunch of Equine Journals at his place, so I'm assuming he, at least, reads those."

"Oh, you've already been to his place, huh? Moving a little fast, aren't we," Karen teased.

Molly sighed. "Clearly I've said too much."

Karen laughed. "I'm only kidding, honey. You're a grown woman – you do whatever you'd like. Just be careful if you know what I mean."

"Okay, I'm hanging up now!" Cried Molly, who was becoming embarrassed. She knew that her mom was just joking though.

"Alright, you have a great day, sweetie. Give me a call later if you want to chat. Love you," Karen said before they hung up.

Molly smiled to herself as she put her cell phone back in her purse. She really was so lucky to have a mom like Karen, truly her best friend, and Molly knew Erin would whole-heartedly agree.

Pouring herself a tall glass of sweet tea and grabbing her *Horse & Style Magazine*, she made her way to the patio outside and repositioned the umbrella so that her chair was in the shade. From this angle, she could see the common ground where renters could walk their dogs, the tree-line behind it where the birds chirped and the squirrels played, and a small pond that was home to many singing crickets. Molly didn't feel like she was in an apartment complex but rather out in the country. It was a lovely, natural setting. Macy had made a nice home for herself in Lexington.

Macy was the kind of person who never let anything bother her, who saw the best in everyone, and who gave one hundred percent in every area of her life.

She had been a brilliant student, a charming daughter and sister, and a great friend. Molly would never forget the day the two met.

It was the first week of second grade and their teacher, Mrs. Bloom, had just dropped the class off at gym. An excellent athlete and someone who never liked to stay in one place for too long, Molly was a fan of gym class, and, as luck would have it, so was Macy.

The class divided into two teams for a rousing game of dodgeball, one of Molly's favorites. As with any second grade class, the action was lively and there was lots of shouting and running, kids darting to and fro as they were getting hit with a ball and then re-entering moments later when a teammate caught a ball. Molly was dodging balls left and right, but her team was dwindling. She paused long enough to look to her right, and there was Macy, the only other player on her team. The rest of her team had been hit and left for the sideline, one by one.

The two young girls looked at each other briefly, nodded, and got down to business, working together to catch one ball after another until their entire team had been reunited back on the floor. Through teamwork, determination, and concentration, they ended up winning the game.

After class, Macy came up to Molly at the water fountain. Macy, wearing a bright purple shirt, flung one of her braided pigtails over her shoulder and smiled directly at her new friend. "Good game. We kicked that other team's butt!"

Molly giggled as she wiped the water off her chin. "We sure did!"

And twenty-one years later, they were still giggling with each other and kicking some butt.

~ Chapter 11 ~

Beau was making notes on a chart and doing his best to stifle a yawn. He hadn't been scheduled to work night shift, but with a colleague out sick and one emergency after another, the hospital had no choice but to call him around four in the morning. His scrubs were wrinkled and dirty with horse hair, horse snot, and a little bit of blood. His left foot had been stepped on three times by two separate horses, and he thought his two little toes were broken. But injuries and grime went with the territory, and he wasn't complaining as, thankfully, all his patients had made it through the night.

He heard laughter behind him. "Tired, huh? I'm not surprised. You dropped my little lady off pretty late last night." He turned around and saw Macy, her eyes twinkling.

Beau smiled as he remembered driving Molly home, holding her hand the whole way. He had prayed the ride would never end. When it did, he walked her up to the door, took her face in his hands and kissed her with more passion and intensity than he had planned. He couldn't help himself. There was just something special about Molly. The way she looked up at him with those angel eyes, with the porch light glowing behind her like a halo – it all felt like a dream. He had never felt this way about a girl so early on.

"Hello? Earth to Beau," Macy laughed as she waved her hand in front of his face. He gave his head a little shake and apologized.

"Sorry, I'm just really tired this morning, got called in just after four o'clock. But yes, I guess I did bring her home a little late. We were just having a really nice time getting to know one another. Molly's very easy to talk to." Beau's eyes again took on a faraway gaze, and Macy knew that he was daydreaming of her best friend. The thought of two wonderful people getting to know one another made her heart swell. They both deserved second chances at love.

After a few minutes of discussing their various patients and treatment options, Macy gathered her files and turned on her heel.

"Oh wait," Beau called after her. "So," he said, clearing his throat and looking at her sheepishly. "Did Molly say anything? About me?"

Macy laughed. "No, I haven't talked to her yet. She was still asleep when I left this morning. But trust me," she said as she started to turn and walk down the hall. "If she hadn't liked you, she would have asked to go home before dinner was even served. That girl doesn't like to waste time!"

Macy said hi to Cassidy who was coming from the opposite direction, heading towards Beau.

"Mornin' Cass," Beau said with a smile.

Cassidy glared at him as she approached, paused for a moment like she was about to say something, but then nodded curtly and continued on.

That's not good, thought Beau. *I hope trouble's not brewin'.*

~~~~~~

Beau knew he should have gone straight to bed after his shift ended, but he wanted to swing by the stable and see Ace. It had been a few days since he'd ridden, and Beau was itching to get out on the trails and do some thinking.

Having heard his truck, Ace was waiting at the gate of his paddock, anxious for some attention. A tall, handsome gelding, Ace was eight years old and as gentle as a lamb. Beau had saved the horse from a bad situation a few years back, and it was as if Ace understood that Beau would always put him first, be his friend. Standing tall at sixteen-three hands and with flashy patches of brown and white, the horse was very handsome.

Beau pulled his western saddle off the rack, carefully threw it over Ace's back, and settled it comfortably on the Navajo print saddle pad that had been a gift from a grateful client. He slipped the bridle over his horse's head and placed the curb bit in his mouth. They were ready to ride.

After Ace had been warmed up properly, Beau let the horse out into a smooth gallop down the wide, weathered trail. He let the horse have his head, and he kept up the blistering pace for a few more strides before he reined him in and turned for home. *Ace loves to run*, Beau thought. *He should have been born a Thoroughbred.*

On the long walk back to the stable, Beau let Ace stretch out and plod happily along, giving his owner plenty of time to think. Beau liked nothing better than to be out in the woods alone with Ace, talking through his troubles.

"What on earth am I getting myself into with Molly?" He mused aloud. "She is smart and beautiful and as sweet as can be. So what's the problem?" Beau shook his head. Was he not ready? The fact that he couldn't get her out of his head told him that, despite his initial thoughts, he probably *was* ready to get back into the swing of things after all.

"I think I'm just afraid of history repeating itself," he said to Ace who flicked an ear back to let Beau know that he was listening. "I know she's not Natalie, but who's to say she won't up and leave just like Natalie did…twice? I don't have time to go through all that again. And Molly's not even from around here. She *is* going to leave and go back home to Maryland."

Beau remembered the first break up with Natalie. It was only one year after undergrad. She was working at one of the larger corporations downtown, and he was in his first year of vet school. They were living in his off-campus housing, a one bedroom apartment with a kitchenette, a tiny bathroom, and a washer and dryer down the hall. But Beau didn't care if space was limited because he was in love. It was their place, and they were making a life of their own.

He had just started doing some research on engagement rings when she came home one night and dropped the bombshell.

"I'm taking a job in L.A." The move hadn't been up for discussion.

And of course he couldn't follow her. They tried to do the long distance thing, but after a few months, they both knew it wasn't going to work. They had chosen their careers.

For four years Beau threw himself into his schoolwork, graduating at the top of his class and landing an internship at Hagyard Medical Center, another prestigious equine hospital in Lexington. He stayed single the entire time. Beau had avoided the whole dating scene at first because his heart had been torn to shreds; then, work became all-consuming. While beautiful women sometimes occupied his bed, they could never claim his heart – it still belonged to Natalie.

And then, just like that, she was back. With Hollywood style and that West Coast glow, she came sweeping back into his life, waltzed into the apartment and declared herself his. Her company had granted her the ability to work remotely, so she flew back to tiny Lexington, Kentucky as fast as she could – or so she said.

They lived together for four more years, moved to a larger apartment to accommodate her gigantic shoe collection, and were happy. Sure, she complained about Beau's long hours at the hospital, and about the smell of horse sweat and manure on his clothes, but she knew his work made him happy.

When he came home covered in grime, she would point him toward the shower, shaking her head in disgust, but would always be waiting in bed.

He should have known something was wrong when she never wanted to discuss marriage, kids, the single family house…a future together. And then one day, just as suddenly as she had reappeared, she was gone. Back to L.A. without much of an explanation. He remembered that heartbreaking moment at the airport, standing there in his cowboy boots and jeans, pleading with her to reconsider. She looked up at him through those huge, starlet sunglasses and smiled a lop-sided, *I wish things could have been different* smile, turned on her heel, and left. That had been just over a year ago.

Ace nickered softly, bringing Beau back to the present.

"Oh yeah? Is that so?" Beau laughed. He loved conversing with his horse, pretending that he understood what Ace said. "You think I should forget about Nat? Go out with Molly, and see where the tide takes me?" Ace flicked another ear. Beau chuckled again. "Well, I guess your advice is as good as anyone's. I agree. Let's see what happens with Molly."

~ Chapter 12 ~

"More inside leg…really push…that's it. Did you feel him bend around your leg? Good. That's perfect. Make another twenty meter circle at C."

Molly was breathing hard as she listened to her instructor and concentrated on every one of Hunter's moves. Since she had decided it was time to look for another horse of her own, she figured it would be wise to get back into top riding form. What Molly hadn't realized was that not only was Barb the owner and barn manager of Fairfield Farm, she was also a dressage instructor. No wonder Macy had chosen to board at this stable. And while Molly had mainly trained and showed in hunter/jumpers, she was just looking to improve her overall fitness, and every little bit helped.

Hunter, the seasoned pro who was practically a schoolmaster, was in his element. He had specifically been bred for dressage and with his powerful neck, elastic gaits, and focused work ethic, it's no surprise that he and Macy had cleaned up at shows.

"Really ask him to extend his trot there…right. Okay at H you can go across your diagonal to F, and then ask him for his right lead canter. Sit back…farther. Good!"

At the end of the lesson, Molly was completely exhausted.

"Oh my," Molly sighed. "I'm really going to feel this one tomorrow. This is night and day from taking a leisurely ride through the trails." She gracefully dismounted by dropping her stirrups and swinging her right leg behind her up and over the cantle of the saddle. Hunter craned his head around to look at Molly, and she praised him lavishly. "Oh you are such a good boy, Hunter! You are the best horse ever!" Molly rolled up her stirrups and then cradled Hunter's head in her arms, scratching him behind his ears.

"You did a fantastic job yourself," Barb smiled. "Was that really the first lesson you've had in four years?"

"At least! I honestly can't remember the last time I rode that hard. But it felt good. I'm so excited to get back into the swing of things. Can I schedule another lesson for the same time next week?"

"Absolutely. I'll mark it on my calendar."

As Molly led Hunter inside the barn, she smiled to herself. Her trip to Kentucky was quickly becoming one of the best ideas she'd ever had. Between Macy and Hunter and Beau, she hadn't given Ty a second thought. Macy's work schedule was perfect. The two girls saw more than enough of each other, but neither felt like the other was in the way. Molly had plenty of time to herself to explore the quaint towns surrounding Lexington, such as Midway, Georgetown, and Versailles, to ride Hunter a few times each week, and to write.

As she led Hunter back into the barn, she happily thought about the routine of her new life. Some mornings Molly would take her laptop outside and sit on the patio while she drank her coffee. It was so peaceful that occasionally she'd tilt her head back, her face toward the sun, and close her eyes. She could hear the birds conversing with one another, feel the breeze on her skin. She was falling in love with Kentucky.

On those mornings she'd respond to emails, check Instagram, and, recently, she had started on the outline of her next book. She wasn't due to have the first draft of it to her agent until the end of the year. Molly hadn't intended on writing much of anything on her Back to Basics trip, but Kentucky had been so inspiring that she found she couldn't help herself. Just thinking of the exquisite landscaping of the stud and breeding farms along Pisgah Pike gave her chills. These farms were their own form of art.

The prospect of doing some serious riding again also made Molly happier than she'd been in a long time. She figured she'd take some dressage lessons with Barb, maybe a few jump lessons at a neighboring farm, and then she'd look for a new horse when she returned home to Maryland. She definitely wanted something green, a project horse she could truly make her own. Thanks to Traveller, she was very partial to Thoroughbreds, so getting a three or four year old off the track was appealing. She knew of plenty of ex-racer placement organizations where she was sure she could find something that fit her requirements. And Molly really liked the idea of giving a Thoroughbred a second chance, a new career. *This summer could, potentially, be one of the best I've ever had*, she thought.

And, of course, there was Beau. He had definitely been unexpected, but she was so glad she met him. He was truly a breath of fresh air in comparison to some of the guys she had dated back home. He wasn't self-centered and pretentious. Beau was kind. He was the definition of southern charm, a gentle soul.

They had been seeing quite a bit of each other over the past week and a half. Meeting in the middle of the trails like they did that first time in the woods, they had gone for a relaxing ride after Beau's day at work. And then, after an especially rough night shift, Beau had called her first thing in the morning and asked her to breakfast. When they met at a local café, Molly was secretly pleased that it was her company Beau had desired after a stressful day at the "office."

And tonight he was having her over for dinner at his place. "I'm not the best cook out there, but I promise you won't leave hungry," he had crooned over the phone when they had spoken the night before.

"Oh you know what that means!" Macy had teased. "He's going to feed you alright, but maybe not the fancy meal you're expecting!"

"Mace! Get your mind out of the gutter!"

Molly had laughed at Macy's humor, but she couldn't help wondering if Beau had any intentions for tonight. She felt so rusty with the whole dating thing.

Conservative by nature, Molly had never been one to sleep around. In fact, she'd only ever slept with her two boyfriends, Erik in college, and Ty most recently.

"Your mom has me a little nervous," Molly said as she led Hunter to the wash stall to be hosed off. "I wonder what Beau's intentions are for tonight."

Finished with his bath, Molly led Hunter outside and released him in his paddock. She could still smell the scent of the apple she had just fed him lingering in the air.

Later that afternoon Molly was taking a walk around the woods by the apartment complex when her sister called.

"Erin!" She yelled when she answered the phone. It had been at least a week since they had connected.

"Moll, what's going on? You've been totally MIA. Is the beautiful Kentucky bluegrass luring you away from me? Or is it this handsome cowboy mom's told me about?" Just like Macy, Erin always got right to the point. Molly was happy to be surrounded by such straight-shooters in her life.

She laughed. "No, the bluegrass is not luring me away. You know I could never leave Maryland for long. I'm too rooted thanks to my *amazing* family," she said with a grin.

"I can't tell if you're being sarcastic or not, but I'll take it. Stay as long as you like, just come home at some point."

"I can handle that."

"So? Tell me what's going on! How's that Dr. Holland of ours? Is she being a good roommate?"

"She's great! She's an excellent roommate. You know Mace, she's a neat freak, so the apartment is immaculate. And since her schedule rotates and she works nights occasionally, we actually end up not seeing each other for a few days. It's just long enough to start missing one another."

"Sounds like a perfect set up. Have you been riding?"

"Sure have. I've been hacking out with Hunter around the barn and through the trails. You would not believe how amazing these trails are. Wide and flat, perfect for a smooth gallop. And I actually took a lesson today, the first one in probably four years. The barn where Macy boards is a pretty high-end dressage barn, so I took a lesson on Hunter."

"I love that horse. He and Mace always made quite the team. So spill. What's the deal with the guy you're dating?"

Molly could hear Erin's smile through the phone and knew she was suppressing a giggle. "Well, I wouldn't exactly say we're *dating* each other, but we have gone out a few times. His name is Beau, and he works with Macy."

"A vet, huh? Fancy! Is he treating you right?"

"Of course. I'm done wasting time on losers." Both of the girls laughed. "He's great though, a really classy guy."

"I'm so happy to hear that. And I hope you two are having some fun – wink, wink!"

Goodness, I'm getting it from all sides, Molly sighed as she shook her head.

~ Chapter 13 ~

Beau had just finished making the iced tea when he heard a knock on the door. Molly was right on time. He opened the door and smiled. Before him stood a rosy-cheeked Molly, fresh-faced and looking lovely in a dark blue jean mini skirt, a coral colored tank top, and a white cardigan with three-quarter length sleeves over top. Her sterling silver earrings sparkled in the sunshine. She looked marvelous.

"Hello," Beau said with a happy smile. "You look like you've had a good day – you're all lit up."

"Thank you. I certainly did! I had my riding lesson today, and it was phenomenal. It felt so great to get a workout in the saddle. I'm not going to lie though, I'm already starting to feel the effects of it. It only took me ten minutes to get here, but my legs had already started to stiffen up. I must be getting old."

"Not old, your muscles are just confused, that's all. They haven't been tasked with that type of workout in a while. After another ride or two, you'll be back to your old self."

He walked over to her, gave her a soft kiss on the lips, and handed her a tall glass of sweet tea.

Molly took a long sip. "This is amazing – is that mint I taste?" She asked while wiping her lips.

"Yes ma'am, it sure is. It's my mama's famous recipe."

"It's delicious," she smiled, her eyes bright. "What's for dinner? Smells amazing."

Beau grinned at her. "Well now you gotta remember, I'm a man. I only know how to cook so many meals. But we're having my favorite: steak, loaded baked potatoes, and broccoli casserole. The casserole is another of mama's recipes."

"Hey, no need to explain. I'm a meat and potatoes kinda girl myself. Is there anything I can do to help?"

"Nope. Everything's almost finished."

While Beau was rinsing a pot in the sink, Molly took the opportunity to sidle up to him. She put her arm around his waist and leaned her head on his shoulder. A fairly tall woman herself, Beau still towered over her. He smelled of cologne and fresh like he had just gotten out of the shower. A hint of leather lingered as well. Molly inhaled his scent and sighed.

Feeling her body wilt against his as she sighed, Beau gently turned her to him and cupped her delicate face in his hands. She stared up at him, so sweet, perfect. She smiled as he moved his face down to meet hers and kissed her passionately. Molly wrapped her arms around his neck and sighed once more. Beau was so hungry for her touch.

Their embrace was cut short by the oven timer, announcing dinner's completion. Within minutes the pair sat at the pre-set table with Beau serving Molly first. Beau asked if Molly cared for any red wine or bourbon but she declined, claiming she much preferred the tea. The steaks were exquisite, juicy and tender; the potatoes, loaded with butter, cheese, bacon bits, and sour cream, were to die for. And between the broccoli casserole and the sweet mint tea, Molly mentioned that Beau's mama must be quite the chef.

"You know," Molly said between bites, "I love potatoes. I could eat some form of potato at every single meal and never tire of them."

"Agreed. I'm always amazed at all those fad diets that have you giving up carbs. I could never do it, not enough willpower I guess."

"Oh my goodness no," Molly protested. "Me neither. I love potatoes and pasta and bread. I'm also a big breakfast eater. I love breakfast for dinner. I'm easy – give me a bowl of instant grits, and I'm a happy camper."

Beau smiled at Molly. How very different she was from Natalie, who ate like a bird. She'd have a pack of cheese and crackers and claim she was stuffed. Molly was just as thin as Nat and clearly wasn't afraid to eat. He liked that.

"Grits are a favorite of mine too, and I remember how much you liked the spoonbread at The Boone Tavern. I'll have to see if I can re-create it from scratch sometime."

"Then I definitely volunteer as taste-tester," she said, smiling at him.

~~~~~~

After dinner they strolled down to the barns, hand-in-hand. West Wind Farm was just a breeding facility, so there were no training stables or training track, just broodmares and babies. Some of the foals with early birthdays had already been weaned and were running around a paddock together, now separated from their mothers.

Molly leaned over the fence as four weanlings swarmed her, shoving their noses in her face, desperate for attention. She laughed. "Wow, what a friendly bunch!" She squealed as one gently nibbled her hair. "Oh

I could just take you all home with me," she crooned as she stroked their faces and fluffed their tiny forelocks.

"Yeah, they get handled all the time. That's one good thing about racehorses. They virtually have constant human interaction from the day they're born. Usually not a shy one in the bunch."

"I know. Traveller, my semi-retired boy, is an ex-racer. I got him straight from the track, and his manners were impeccable. I don't think I'll ever own another breed of horse. Trav has turned me onto a life-long love affair with Thoroughbreds. Ha – they're full of energy, aren't they?" She marveled as the pack of weanlings took off streaking around their field, bucking and pawing the air, sunfishing and jumping over invisible oxers. They were clearly showing off for their audience.

"When do you think you'll get another horse?"

"I'll probably start seriously looking the moment I get back home. But I can't resist. I've already been on the CANTER and New Vocations websites. They have some good-looking prospects."

Beau's heart felt a sharp pang at the mention of her going home to Maryland and leaving him behind. He wasn't sure what he expected her to say though. It's not like she was going to stick around for him. They'd only known each other a few weeks. He quickly changed the subject.

"So what are your plans for the fourth?"

"Oh my goodness, it's July already, isn't it? I can't believe it. I actually don't have any plans." She smiled at him sweetly. "What do y'all do 'round here for fun on the fourth?" She drawled. Her silly behavior melted Beau, and he reached for Molly and held her close. She whispered in his ear, "It's my favorite holiday."

Beau whispered back, holding her head in his hand, softly running his fingers through her silky hair, "Oh is it? Well then I guess we'll have to think of somethin' real special."

~ Chapter 14 ~

"So, did you do it?" Macy asked first thing the following morning. Both girls were standing in the kitchen in their pajamas clutching large mugs of coffee.

"Well good morning to you too!" Molly replied. She shook her head as she turned to grab a bowl for her cereal. Then she laughed. She expected no less from her best friend.

Macy continued, a smile spreading across her face. "I'm just saying, you got in late last night. And he cooked you a romantic dinner. Sometimes one thing leads to another, nothing to be ashamed about."

Molly sighed as she poured her Honeynut Cheerios. She looked up at Macy and shook her head. "No, for your information, we did not *do it*. I thought it might lead there, but then he got called into work."

"Oh rats! He was on call last night, wasn't he? Talk about cruddy timing. But tell me everything. I want details."

Knowing there was no way to avoid this conversation, Molly came right out with it. She told Macy about Beau's dinner, complete with broccoli casserole and mint sweet tea. She recounted their post-meal walk outside around the grounds of the farm and even included the adorable weanlings playing tag in their field.

"And...? No offense, just get to the good stuff," Macy said, motioning her hand in a hurry-it-up sort of way.

"I'm getting there! And hey – what about you? How come I don't get to hear the juicy details of your love life?"

Macy groaned. "What love life? I work too much to meet people. I'm thinking about going on one of those dating sites though."

"Good idea! I think you should. I have a friend back home who's had quite a bit of success with them. She's actually engaged now to…"

"Hey!" Macy interrupted. "I know what you're doing. Quit changing the subject and dish. I'm living vicariously through you." She winked at her.

Molly laughed, "Okay, okay," she said defeated. She continued on to tell Macy about her and Beau's passionate kiss outside by the weanlings' field and how they quickly took their passion back into the house.

As they walked through the back door, Beau took Molly's hand and led her to the living room where he sat on the couch and pulled her onto his lap. How long they stayed like that, holding each other and kissing softly, Molly couldn't recall. "I think he was just getting ready to take me into the bedroom when his beeper went off," Molly sighed. She didn't tell Macy that she had been more of the aggressor at that moment, taking off her shirt and then unbuttoning Beau's. She had surprised even herself at how badly she had wanted him.

"Ugh, I would have died." Macy was incredulous as if it had happened to her.

"Yeah, it was beyond frustrating, but I understood. Beau has an important job, and I would never want to come between him and a horse in need."

Macy smiled a knowing, satisfied smile. "I'd say you two are pretty perfect for each other."

~~~~~

Later that morning Molly received an email from Beau thanking her for being so understanding about his having to go into work the previous night.

Molly,

I want to apologize for last night. I probably shouldn't have even had you over knowing that I was on call, but I can never pass up an opportunity to see you. Not everyone would have been as understanding about my work, and I appreciate that. You are a true horse lover, and for that I'm grateful. Hopefully we won't be interrupted the next time.

I also wanted to say how happy I've been getting to know you these last few weeks. You have been a breath of fresh air to this tired, broken man, and I hope we can continue to see each other while you're in Kentucky. And when you're not...well, I'd like to talk about that too.

It's supposed to be a beautiful day – go take Hunter out for a spin! I'll be calling you later tonight to discuss some plans for the 4th, your favorite holiday.

Yours,
Beau

Molly smiled to herself. This was the first time Beau had ever emailed her, and she realized that there was one line in particular that made her ecstatic. "And when you're not...well, I'd like to talk about that, too."

Did he want to get serious, make their relationship official? *I can't believe all this is really happening...and so soon*, she sighed happily.

Molly had seen the disappointment flutter briefly in Beau's eyes when she had mentioned looking for a horse the moment she got home to Maryland, but she had chalked it up to her imagination.

But she had been right. He wants to be with her too.

Giddy with excitement, she went about the rest of her morning routine, cleaned her room a little, and dressed for the day. While she wanted to take Hunter for a nice, relaxing hack, Macy had left earlier to do just that. She was glad that Macy still made time in her hectic schedule to hang out with her sweet boy.

Instead, Molly decided that she would go shopping as she had realized yesterday that she was basically out of clothes. She hadn't anticipated meeting Beau, or anyone for that matter, and needing nice, date-type clothes. Instead, she had packed a variety of riding attire, simple shorts and t-shirts, lounge-wear, and yoga pants. Most of the more presentable clothes she had been wearing belonged to Macy. Her best friend was kind enough to open her home to her all summer, but she didn't have to open her closet, too. Molly didn't want to keep taking advantage of her by stealing her clothes for the next two months.

As Molly drove through the rolling Kentucky countryside, she viewed her surroundings with a new perspective. Would this town be her new home? Could she move here for Beau? Was it too soon to start thinking like this? While she loved Lexington and felt completely welcomed and at home here among like-minded horse people, she wasn't sure if she could ever leave Maryland. She was an east-coaster through and through. *Besides, mom would kill me*, she thought as she laughed to herself.

Molly made her way from store to store and was reminded again at how much she hated shopping. Chalking it up as a necessary evil, she forced herself to continue on until she had purchased two sundresses, three summery blouses, a pair of white slacks, a bathing suit and cover-up, sandals, and a pair of too large, almost comical looking sunglasses. She also bought three new pairs of earrings and some chunky bangle bracelets. Molly wasn't much of a jewelry person, but she figured it was time to invest in some new bling.

On her way home, she passed Wallace Station and decided to stop for a late lunch where she ordered the East Hampton Hot Ham & Brie sandwich. She found it interesting that Guy Fieri from The Food Network had featured the little deli on Diners, Drive-Ins & Dives. The small restaurant definitely had the look of one of those hidden, local gems.

As she sat on the shaded deck behind the restaurant eating her delicious sandwich, she thought about Beau and wondered what he had planned for the Fourth of July. She hadn't been lying when she told him it was her favorite holiday.

People were always surprised to hear that Christmas or Thanksgiving, the two most popular, weren't her favorites, but she couldn't help it. There was just something magical about the Fourth that had always captivated her, especially as a child. For Molly, it truly meant the start of the summer, her favorite season. She loved the holiday for its rituals: the local town parade and festivities, the large cook-out at her parents' house, and the fireworks at dusk. It had been a time to be young and carefree and not think about school. It was a day to celebrate the birth of the great nation she so loved.

It was a day that led the way for one exciting time after another. There had been horse shows to attend and vacations to take. She'd have her friends over for pool parties where they'd splash the day away in the hot sun. It meant sleepovers where she'd stay up late with her friends telling ghost stories and talking about their latest crushes. The Fourth symbolized summer at its finest. Molly wished she could stop time and live in those precious moments forever.

She also enjoyed being home full-time with her mother and sister. With her dad at the office all day, it was girl time, all the time. They'd wake early and care for the horses, sometimes taking a sunrise ride before the heat of the day was upon them. Then they'd hop into the car to help their mother run errands, or they'd help with farm chores. Occasionally, they treated themselves to pedicures at the local salon.

In the afternoon, they'd have lunch on the patio and lounge by the pool, soaking up the free time that only summer allows. When her father got home from work, they'd gather around the table on the patio for a pleasant dinner outside, usually prepared on the grill. Molly wistfully wished those days had never ended.

And while the dynamic of her favorite holiday and season had changed, she still looked forward to this time of year. She couldn't wait to add Beau to her to list of happy summer memories.

~ Chapter 15 ~

Beau had debated with himself all night about sending that email to Molly. He didn't want to come across as too forward, but he wanted her to know how he felt about their relationship, whatever it was at this point. He knew he was being a little forthright in saying that he wanted to talk about what would happen after she left Kentucky, but he didn't care. Something had happened to him during the past few weeks, and he was tired of playing it safe. The only thing he was beating himself up about was not saying that to her in person. Last night would have been the perfect opportunity.

As he drove home from his shift, he marveled at how willing Molly had been the previous evening. When he held her in his arms, all he had wanted to do was take her back to his bedroom and make love to her, but he didn't want to rush it. He was shocked when Molly pulled away, stood up in front of him, and began to undress. Her cardigan and her shirt fell to the floor. Then she leaned in and started unbuttoning his shirt, one button at a time, tantalizingly slow. Her eyes, when they made contact with his, had taken on a shade deep and dark. His heart had exploded inside his chest.

Then his damn beeper went off. He could not believe it. He looked at the end table where the device was rattling around, and then looked back at Molly with what he knew were probably crazed, deer-in-headlight eyes. But she just gave him that lop-sided smile, sighed a little, and told him to check it out. It's like she's some sort of angel.

He knew he was still worked up and flustered as he drove to the hospital and started his shift. A colleague gave him a searching look but didn't say anything.

Later that night he started thinking about how Natalie had reacted when his beeper had interrupted them, which it had, many times over, as that's the nature of his job. She would first ask him to ignore it and try to pin herself on top of him, forcing him to have to gently push her off and choose the horses over her, again and again. Every time it happened, she grew more and more distant. Beau would never forget what Natalie had said the last time they had been interrupted, and he had to leave for work.

"You know those horses are killing us." She had said matter-of-factly, staring off into the distance.

He held out his arms and shrugged. "There's nothing I can do about it," he said sadly.

She turned to him and held his gaze for a few moments before she said, almost resolutely, "I know."

And yet he was still surprised that day she had packed up and left. *I guess that's what happens when horse people and non-horse people try to have a relationship*, Beau thought.

But Molly – she was another story. There had been no malice in her eyes when the beeper sounded, no frustration. Just full understanding and compassion. She had even told him to rush for fear of the horse that was in trouble. He would make it up to her though. Beau was off for the next few days and wasn't on call either. It was a miracle.

After a quick nap that afternoon, Beau headed down to the barn to see Ace. The well-behaved gelding was in his stall, snoozing lightly behind the fan that was attached to his gated door. He awoke when he heard Beau's footsteps and let out a soft whinny.

"Well hello to you too," Beau said as he reached his hand out to scratch behind Ace's ears. The horse leaned into his caresses and slowly closed his eyes. "You like that now, don't you?" He asked.

Out on the trails Beau let the reins hang loose, letting Ace pick his path, and he let his thoughts loose, too. What if she asked him to go back with her to Maryland? Could he do that? Beau loved Kentucky, loved its perfect, rolling countryside, its people. It was a special land all its own, a land he had called home for many years now. He had always thought that if he left his beloved bluegrass state, it would be to head home to Georgia. But going home for good just hadn't appealed to him.

Maryland. He had never been there. He'd been to Washington, D.C., which was close, but that was it. When he had driven north from Georgia to visit Peter in Alexandria, Virginia, one summer in between their junior and senior years of college, Beau had played the part of tourist, but he had never ventured north of D.C.

When Beau asked if there was anything to do or see in Maryland, Peter shook his head. "Not really, unless we head out to Annapolis or up to Baltimore, but neither is very close, especially with traffic."

But Molly spoke beautifully about her hometown, Monkton. She described it as "true Maryland horse country," but said that it still didn't compare to Lexington as this town was completely devoted to the horse. But apparently when Molly would go foxhunting, she'd ride right off of her parents' property and join the hunt. It did sound pretty amazing, and Beau wished that he would have a chance to see it. But permanently? He wasn't sure.

But how was it fair then to ask Molly to stay in Lexington? *I still can't believe I'm thinking like this*, he thought to himself.

~~~~~~

Later that afternoon he gave Molly a call.

"Hey darlin', whatcha been up to?" He drawled.

"I just got back from shopping," Molly moaned. "I *hate* shopping. There's nothing appealing about it whatsoever."

Beau laughed. Molly and Natalie, who could spend an entire day at the mall, couldn't be more opposite if they tried. "So I'm not sure if you've talked to Macy about the Fourth, but I was thinking we'd all head into town for the parade. I remember you said you enjoyed the parade back home and think this one will probably be similar. All small towns are alike."

Molly could hear the smile in Beau's voice. "Absolutely! I love a good parade."

"Excellent. And then I was thinkin' we'd head back to the farm here. The Richardsons always have a huge BBQ and fish fry. Macy and a few colleagues came with me last year, so I'm going to invite them all again."

"A fish fry? I've never been to one of those. We have crab feasts back in Maryland, but I'm up for whatever as long as we see some fireworks somewhere later that night. Even backyard fireworks work for me."

"Then it's a date. The parade, fish fry, and fireworks."

"Sounds like a perfect Fourth."

~ Chapter 16 ~

The parade was fun, just like Molly's local one back home. There were handmade floats advertising the local churches, Boy Scout troops, and 4-H clubs. Four marching bands mingled throughout the procession, and, of course, there were quite a few horses and riders, decked out in their patriotic finery, strutting their stuff along the street. The horses had streamers laced in their manes and tails, with red, white, and blue glitter on their hooves.

Later that afternoon, she and Macy were sitting under the shade of a massive, hundred year old oak tree watching the BBQ festivities. There were people and food and excitement everywhere you looked. Beau was off chatting with some neighboring friends.

Molly took a long gulp from her water bottle. "This is awesome. I love backyard gatherings like this. I can't believe it's so crowded though!"

"I know, right?" Macy agreed. "The Richardsons do this every year. And you are so funny, by the way. Did I really hear you tell the host that you were a *fish fry virgin*?"

Molly laughed so hard she almost snorted water through her nose. "Yes! I can't believe I said that. Poor Beau must think I'm crazy. Sometimes I just can't control what comes out of my mouth. That fish was so good though."

Macy smiled over at her best friend. "I'm so happy you're here. You look like you're having the time of your life, but are you missing home at all?"

"I will say it's a little strange to be spending the Fourth somewhere other than Monkton. Mom called the other day and asked if I could come home for the holiday and then go back. I felt bad, but I told her I was not trekking through the hills of West Virginia any more than I had to."

Macy shook her head. "Your poor mother, she just misses you."

"I know, and I miss her too. But I said if I was going to spend the Fourth away from home, this was the best place to be – in the middle of gorgeous horse country with my best friend."

"And Beau, your *boyfriend*!" Macy started to giggle.

Molly picked up a small stick from the ground and threw it at Macy. "You are impossible! He is not my boyfriend…at least I don't think so. I have no idea what we are." Molly deliberately hadn't told Macy of Beau's remark about wanting to talk about what would happen after she left Kentucky. She wanted to keep that to herself for right now.

"Hey, how's Gypsy doing?" Molly asked, trying to change the subject.

"I know you're just trying to change the subject, but I'll let you just this once. Gypsy still isn't progressing the way we'd like, not for her to go back into training. It's starting to look like she won't ever be a racehorse."

"What do you think will happen to her?" Molly was worried about her beautiful, four-legged friend. She had visited with her a few times over the past weeks and was growing quite fond of the friendly filly.

"That's up to her owners. Hopefully they'll place her with someone who wants to train her as a regular riding horse, for which she'd be perfect. She just won't hold up under the intense training she'll need as a racehorse."

"When will you know for sure whether she's going to go back into racing or not?"

"We basically know now, but the owners are being a little stubborn. They decided to they want to give her more time. Which is fine, but they need to be realistic, especially since the hospital stay is costing them a fortune. But I guess when you have that much money, it doesn't matter."

Molly was quiet for a few moments. "When you find out for sure what's going on with her, can you let me know? If they'd like to find her a home, I'd be willing to take her."

Macy squealed. "Really? That would be awesome! It's about time you got another horse!"

"I know, I know. I had wanted to wait until I got home to find one, but she's here and she may need a home – so why not? I can have her shipped back east."

Macy was grinning from ear to ear. "You absolutely can! Oh I'm so excited for you!"

"Well don't get too excited yet. Who knows what the owners will want to do." But Molly was already thinking about how she'd get Gypsy home and when she would start her retraining. She prayed that the owners didn't have anyone else lined up to take her. She'd be devastated if that was the case.

Beau wandered over a few minutes later. Molly patted the grass next to her. "Here, pull up a chair," she said with a smile.

"Why thank you, fish fry virgin. Don't mind if I do," he grinned as he sat next to her.

The three of them chatted for a bit and it was decided that Molly and Macy would head home to shower and change, and Beau would be along later to pick them up for the fireworks.

~~~~~

"What do you mean you're not going?" Molly asked incredulously.

"I lied. I want you two to have some alone time, so I'm staying here. Besides, I have to work tomorrow. Some jackass named Beau is taking a few vacation days, so I have to cover for him." Macy winked at her friend.

"But I want you to come. You love fireworks." Molly felt like a little kid about to throw a tantrum.

"I do love fireworks, but not as much as I love you. Go get into his truck and have some fun tonight." Molly started to protest but Macy cut her off. "Go! He's waiting!" And she shooed her out the door and closed it before Molly could protest anymore.

Molly climbed into Beau's truck and shook her head. "That brat," she said.

"Everything okay?" Beau asked, looking concerned.

"Oh everything is fine. Macy wants us to have some alone time and wouldn't come even when I begged her. Brat." Of course Molly wanted to be alone with Beau, but she didn't want Macy to feel unwelcome.

Beau laughed. "That girl is somethin' else."

"Oh yeah, she's something alright." Molly said, and then laughed to herself.

There was always something about watching fireworks that made Molly nostalgic. As she leaned against Beau as they sat in the bed of his truck, she thought about other fireworks displays with other people, other boyfriends. Those memories seemed like a lifetime ago, and she had to stop herself from thinking about life and how it went too fast and how time kept marching forward.

A year ago she never would have imagined she'd be in Lexington, Kentucky, for the Fourth of July, wrapped tightly in Beau's strong arms. *Life definitely throws some curveballs*, Molly thought reflectively.

"Which one is your favorite?" Molly asked, breaking the silence.

"Favorite what? Firework?" Beau asked. Molly nodded. "Well, I'm not sure. I've never thought about it before."

"Really? You've never thought about it? Well, maybe you're the normal one; maybe I'm crazy for putting so much thought into fireworks. When I was five, I told my mom I wanted to *be* a firework." She could feel Beau smile, and he leaned down, smoothed her hair, and kissed her head. She was *his* little firework.

"So which one is your favorite?" Beau asked.

"I like the thin white ones that burst out like palm trees and then fall down towards the earth like a weeping willow. They stay lit the longest, fading slowly. Do you know which ones I mean?"

"I certainly do. I didn't realize I was dating a firework aficionado," Beau said.

They were silent for a few moments. Beau cleared his throat.

"Well, I hope that we're dating. Lately I've been thinking of you as my girlfriend."

Molly turned so she could face Beau. She cradled his head in her hands and brought his face down to meet hers. They kissed softly for a few moments. "I like that you've been thinking that way," Molly said when they broke apart.

Beau told her that he was afraid to say anything earlier for fear of scaring her off. After all, she did come west to get a break from men and relationships. Then he was worried because he knew that her trip would come to an end, and that she'd pack up, kiss him good-bye, and return home.

"But I realized, and I hope you're thinking along the same lines, that just because your trip ends doesn't mean we have to end. I'm not sure what we'll do, but we can make it work." Beau said quietly. He was holding his breath, waiting for her response.

"You're right. We'll figure everything out. We don't need all the answers tonight. And besides, I'm not going anywhere any time soon." Molly pressed herself against him, kissing him once again.

Beau kissed her back fiercely, struggling to maintain his composure. "Would you like to head back to my place?" He asked breathlessly.

"Yes," she replied.

~ Chapter 17 ~

The drive home seemed to take forever. They had left just before the grand finale, and were able to beat most of the traffic, but the roads still seemed endless.

When they burst into the dark house, Molly grabbed onto Beau tightly, and he pulled her close.

"Your beeper's off, right?" She asked with a sly grin on her face.

"Hell yeah it is."

In one smooth motion, Beau scooped Molly up in his arms and carried her to his room. He laid her on the bed and kissed her again. She reached up and pulled his shirt off, revealing his tan, chiseled chest, and she ran her hands up his chest and over his muscled shoulders.

"Do you have something? I'm not on the pill anymore."

"Yeah," Beau replied. "I'll be right back." He walked over to his closet and pulled out a condom from a shoe box on the floor. Molly was sitting upright against the headboard, looking pensive. "Are you okay? Look, sweetheart, we don't have to do this if it's not what you want."

Molly smiled warmly at this kind and gentle man. "Of course it's what I want, it's just that," she paused and looked away. He turned her chin until they made eye contact.

"What is it?"

Molly took a breath. "It's been a while since I've done this. A long while." She gave him a little smile.

Beau let out a breath and spoke softly. "We'll take it nice and slow then, sound good?"

With that Molly's eyes darkened deep and lustful. She began to unbutton her blouse and let it fall to the floor, revealing a white cotton bra. Beau reached forward and unzipped her shorts, exposing matching underwear. He loved Molly's simplicity. She was sexy without even trying; she didn't need fancy lingerie or lacy thongs. The white underwear made her long, tan legs glow, and he could hardly contain himself.

But he forced himself to relax and take it slow. Molly reached for his belt and unbuckled it with ease, pulling it off slowly and dropping it to the ground.

Once the rest of their clothes had melted away, he pulled back from Molly's kiss and asked her one last time if she was sure. Her answer came as an action. She grabbed the condom on the nightstand, unwrapped it, and rolled it on for him. Then she took a hold and slid him inside her.

~~~~~~

Molly awoke the next morning in Beau's arms. She rolled over and laid her head on his chest and smiled up at the man who had just given her one of the best nights she'd had in a long while. Beau was awake and smiled back as he ran his hand through her hair and cupped her chin.

"For someone who said she was out of practice, you certainly didn't act like it." Beau laughed to himself as Molly pinched his arm.

They had fallen asleep shortly after they had made love only to wake a few hours later for a repeat performance. Actually, it was Molly who woke and got Beau stirring again. She didn't know what had come over her, but she didn't care. Beau made her feel like she could do, say, or be anything. He made her feel so beautiful, like she was perfect and had nothing to hide. She couldn't remember the last time someone had made her feel this completely safe, free from her inhibitions. She liked the Molly she was when she was with him.

They laid together for some time, holding each other and talking, until their stomachs began to growl. Only then did they begrudgingly climb out of bed and dress. While Beau fixed them a hearty breakfast of eggs, pancakes, bacon, and grits, Molly checked her phone.

"Listen to this – it's a text from Macy." Molly read it out loud.

You didn't come home last night, so I'm assuming you'll have some exciting news to share. However, just so I don't worry that some lunatic kidnapped you at the fireworks, please respond so I know you're okay. Love you, you wild woman you!

Beau was laughing as he brought Molly's coffee to the table. "Macy is one of a kind. But she's a good friend, nice of her to check in."

"She's the best. I just told her that I'm alive and very well – we'll catch up tonight." Molly's eyes twinkled as she emphasized the word, *very*.

Beau stood before Molly and held her chin in his hand while he caressed her cheek with his thumb. "You," he said staring straight into her eyes, "are also one of a kind, and I can't tell you how happy I am to have you in my life."

Molly couldn't quite tell, but she thought she saw Beau's eyes glisten for just a moment. She grabbed his hand in hers and lowered her head to kiss his palm. "I feel the same way, Beau. I feel like I'm living in a dream."

~ Chapter 18 ~

Macy was sitting at her desk updating charts when Cassidy walked up. Normally the two girls got along pretty well, but lately Cassidy had been acting funny, and their easy chatter was strained and forced.

"Good afternoon," Macy said as Cassidy approached. "Did you have a nice Fourth?"

Cassidy had a sour look on her face. It was obvious that something had upset her. "Not really. I went to the Club with my parents for some tennis and swimming. But that was about it, pretty boring. What did you do?"

"Oh the usual, the parade in town and then the fish fry at the Richardsons' in the afternoon. Other than being incredibly hot, it was a really great day."

"So what's up with Beau? Are he and your bestie officially together now?" She emphasized *bestie*. Macy had no idea why Cass was being so rude, but, of course, she had no idea that Beau and Cassidy had spent time together outside of work.

"I'm not completely sure, but I think so." She figured Molly and Beau discussed this particular matter last night, and she was anxious to know the final verdict. The fact that Molly had stayed out all night was a good sign that her best friend wouldn't need one of those dating sites any time soon.

Cassidy sighed. "Don't you think this is all a waste of time? I mean, she's going back to Maryland at some point, isn't she?"

Macy didn't like her tone, nor did she understand why Cass was so concerned with Beau's love life. She had gotten the impression over the last few months that

Cass was into Beau, but that made no sense to her. Not only was he a colleague, he was one of their supervisors. That was like playing with fire. Macy wanted to tell her to start acting like a professional, but instead she turned her attention back to her charts and answered casually.

"They're adults. They can do whatever they want."

She heard Cassidy sigh again, louder this time, and stalk off. *Did she think I was going to side with her over a matter we shouldn't even be discussing at work anyway?* Macy shook her head and silently prayed that she and Cass would be on different shifts for as long as possible.

~~~~~

It was mid-afternoon by the time Beau had returned from dropping Molly off at Macy's apartment. They had agreed they would meet up later for dinner after they showered and changed.

Beau couldn't believe his luck, and when he passed the mirror hanging in his hallway, he realized that he was smiling. And he just couldn't stop. He couldn't believe that he had met Molly, that she was a real, living person and not some fictional character he dreamt up. She was everything he had been searching for.

Beau, realizing he was starving, strolled into the kitchen to make himself a BLT and pour a glass of water. As he was munching on the sandwich and some chips, his cell phone rang. The caller ID showed it was his older brother, Tate.

"Hey bro, how are ya?" Beau answered heartily.

"Hey Beau. Doin' okay," Tate answered in a voice that did not display his usual pep. Something was wrong. "Hey I don't want to worry you, but thought that you should know – dad's in the hospital with some chest pain. He just thinks it's a bad case of indigestion, but mom wanted them to run some tests."

Beau sighed deeply into the phone. Since his father's initial heart trouble last year, Beau had constantly worried about his dad. "Should I come down? I can be there by late evening."

"Oh no, no need to come down, at least I don't think so. Why don't you stay put for now, and I'll call as soon as the tests come back. Annie's at the hospital now, so mama and dad aren't alone." Annie was Beau's older sister, the sassy middle child of their family.

Tate hung up shortly thereafter, promising to call as soon as he knew something. It was moments like this that Beau felt riddled with guilt for not living close to his aging parents. Tate and his wife, Belle, and Annie and her husband, Michael, all lived within a five mile radius of each other.

It wasn't that Beau didn't like Georgia – he did. But Kentucky had always felt more like home with its horse fanatics and its easy ways. However, maybe it was time to think about moving home, especially with his father's ailing health. There was nothing in life more important than family, so why had he separated himself from his for so long?

Before he knew it, he was imagining taking Molly home to meet his mama and dad. He could picture how beautiful she'd look hugging his mama for the first time, the warmth in her eyes and touch. Molly was as genuine as the setting sun.

And his family would be so good to her. His mama, for one, would be beside herself that not only had her youngest found someone to love, but that he had moved back home. Her family would be together again. Beau loved the thought of how that would make her cry happy tears of joy.

Annie would befriend Molly instantly. Annie, with her quick tongue and even quicker smile, reminded Beau of Macy. He was sure that Molly would see the similarity and find comfort in that friendship. And Tate, his big brother, was the person whom he had looked up to for his entire life. It would be nice to see him on a daily basis, Beau admitted to himself. And, after all, there were horses in Georgia.

But could he really leave everything behind and move back? Would Molly follow him? Life down south was similar to Kentucky, slow and steady, night and day from the rat race up north. Would Molly be bored?

Beau shook his head as he came out of his daydream and back into reality. *So many questions*, he thought to himself. So much ambiguity. But he knew one thing for certain. He needed Molly in his life.

~ Chapter 19 ~

It was quarter of six when Beau knocked on Molly's door. They had decided to have dinner in town at The Julep Cup, one of Beau's favorite restaurants. Molly was a heavenly vision when she answered the door. She was wearing a red and white striped top with crisp white pants. Her hair had been curled and hung loose in tousled waves around her face and down her back. Shiny silver hoop earrings completed the look.

"Wow," Beau said. "You look gorgeous – your hair is beautiful." He couldn't take his eyes off her. Her eye shadow glittered when she moved her head, making her hazel eyes shine.

Molly blushed just the tiniest shade of red. "Thanks, Macy told me to curl it. She said it was time you saw a different look on me," Molly said as she laughed and rolled her eyes at the same time.

The Julep Cup was exquisite. The interior, like most restaurants in Lexington, was horse-themed, and the main dining area was classy and sophisticated with dark maroon-colored walls and various equestrian accoutrements like bits and bridles and horse show ribbons adorning the walls. Molly loved it.

Over an appetizer of homemade bourbon barrel beer cheese, Beau told Molly about his father's visit to the hospital. "I spoke with my mama while I was on my way to pick you up. All the tests came back fine, so they're releasing him tonight." Beau's relief was obvious.

"Oh that's wonderful news. So then it was just a bad case of heartburn?" Molly asked.

"They don't know for sure, but that's what they're thinking. Mama said dad's acting just as stubborn and feisty as ever, so he must be feeling okay," Beau said with a smile.

They sat in silence for a few minutes, munching on their cheese and crackers. Then Beau cleared his throat and looked directly into Molly's eyes. "I just want you to know that last night was one of the best nights I've had in a long time...hell, maybe ever." Molly's eyes met Beau's and they were shining again. "I'm not sure what the future holds for us, sweetheart, but I'm not sure I can imagine one without you in it."

Molly swallowed hard and nodded. "I feel the same way," she said, barely above a whisper. Then she gave a lop-sided grin. "Sometimes I feel like we must be moving too fast to feel this way already, but I don't think we are." She was silent for a moment. "I've actually been thinking about it a lot, and no matter how you slice it, someone has to move. Either you come back with me to Maryland, or I move to Kentucky. Or," she paused, "we both move to Georgia. I hadn't really considered that as an option, but I guess it should be on the table." She couldn't believe they were having this conversation so soon. Hadn't they just met?

"Do you have a preference?" Beau asked hesitantly.

"Well, of course I want you to come to Maryland because it's my home, and I absolutely love it there. And my family – we're just so close. But I'm a writer. I can work anywhere. You have a career at Rood & Riddle. You're established. It would be easiest for me to move here to Lexington." Molly paused and shook her head. "I can't believe we're having this discussion already. Beau, are we crazy?" She asked pleadingly.

Beau shook his head firmly and reached across the table, taking her hands in his. "I've been asking myself that question as well and the conclusion I've come to is that no, darlin', we're not crazy. We're two people who found love when we least expected it. Because, Molly, I love you. I think I started falling in love with you that first day I met you out on the trails. I've just been afraid to tell you."

Molly smiled that sweet, genuine smile of hers and said, "Oh Beau, I love you, too. I wanted to say it yesterday, but was afraid it would sound too cliché and ruin the night."

Beau tilted his head back and laughed heartily. "Sweetheart, it wouldn't have ruined the night, but I'm laughing because I wanted to say it too and thought the very same thing. I guess great minds really do think alike."

At that moment the waiter came over with their meals and the two reluctantly let go of each other's hands. Molly had ordered the shrimp and grits, and Beau ordered his usual at this restaurant, the traditional Kentucky Hot Brown, which was oven-roasted turkey and ham on sourdough bread, smothered with mornay sauce and cheese with a tomato and bacon on top.

Their food was absolutely delicious, and Molly commented that the restaurant definitely rivaled The Boone Tavern where they had dined on their first date.

They were too full to contemplate dessert and ordered two coffees instead.

"So what are we going to do?" Molly asked as she stirred some cream and two sugars into her coffee.

"Well, you were going to stay for most of the summer anyway, right? I say we stick to the original plan.

You stay with Macy, and then towards the end of the summer, we'll make some decisions. If you decide to stay in Lexington, you are more than welcome to move in with me. And in the meantime, if you'd like me to see what kinds of veterinarian positions are available in Maryland, I will because, darlin', I will follow you wherever you go."

Molly's heart melted, and she thought about how much she loved this man already. Life worked so mysteriously. "For now, I think it would be easier for us to just stay here, but I appreciate your willingness to consider Maryland too."

Later that night, Beau took Molly back to his house where he made love to her again, gently and passionately as if thanking her for agreeing, at least for the time being, to stay in Kentucky with him. He didn't think he'd ever been happier.

~ Chapter 20 ~

Just like back home, August in Kentucky dawned hazy, hot, and humid. Morning coffee on the patio became a thing of the past as Molly had retreated indoors where the poor air conditioner plugged away non-stop. It was officially time she started on her next novel, and she was surprised at how quickly she had finished the outline and started on the first draft. This book would be slightly autobiographical as it took place in Lexington and the main character was visiting relatives for the summer, taking a break from her gloomy life in Boston.

She picked Boston because it was one of her favorite cities since she and her family had vacationed there and to the surrounding New England towns regularly during Molly's childhood. It was a city she knew well, a city she could describe and bring to life on her blank pages. She couldn't choose Baltimore as then it really might become the story of her life!

July had been an exquisitely wonderful month, and Molly had passed the lazy days hanging out with Macy, Beau, and Hunter. She was riding regularly, mixing trail rides and dressage lessons with Hunter, and he seemed to be enjoying every minute of the attention.

Molly had also begun taking a weekly jumping lesson at another local farm and was surprised that her form hadn't deteriorated too much. She was riding a fifteen year old Thoroughbred who was both a seasoned eventer and a lesson horse for advanced riders. His name was Zeke and he, like Hunter, was a perfect gentleman and truly loved his job.

Earlier in the week, her jumping instructor had surprised her by trailering Zeke into the Kentucky Horse

Park. Their famous cross country course was open to the public that day, so they were able to get in a fantastic schooling session. In the past, Molly had focused on hunter equitation and show jumping, but she was starting to get the eventing bug and decided that her next prospect needed to be brave enough to tackle the sturdy fences on cross country. Even some of the low-level, local events she'd watched Erin compete in had tricky jump combinations.

After a few weeks of lessons and harder riding, Molly finally felt like she was back in shape, fit enough to start training a youngster. She was devastated, however, to learn that Gypsy's owners had taken her home and were contemplating keeping her to be a broodmare. While her racing career was over before it started, she was incredibly well-bred, so her owners wanted to hold onto her for a bit.

Of course, by the time this decision was made, Molly had truly fell in love with the little filly and was crossing her fingers that she would become hers. Beau had held Molly when she cried over the news that Gypsy had gone back home, but he promised that he would reach out to her owners periodically to see if they had changed their minds. At only two years of age, Gypsy's owners felt that the filly was too young to be bred, so, Beau had said, the owners may decide not to wait that long after all.

Molly prayed that they would change their minds and put the sweet filly up for adoption. Her owners had assured Beau that he and Molly would have first right of refusal should that happen. Still hoping for the best, Molly had decided to hold off on horse shopping until there was a more definitive answer. In the meantime, she still had Hunter and now Zeke.

And, of course, there was Beau. He and Molly had continued to grow together as a couple, and while they still hadn't made any decisions about their living situation, both felt relieved that they were on the same page. The end of Molly's trip wouldn't be the end of their relationship.

In mid-July, had Beau asked Molly to come along with him to Louisville to meet his best friend, Peter, his wife, and their children. Molly had been overjoyed to meet one of Beau's longtime friends, and she took an instant liking to the energetic man who had known Beau for many years. With his striking personality and interesting fashion sense, it was difficult to imagine that he and Beau had been so close. But within five minutes of seeing the old duo together, Molly could see that they had a lot in common and complemented each other very well. They reminded her of herself and Macy.

Peter and his family lived in the suburbs, but Beau drove her by Churchill Downs so she could see the famous racetrack that is home to the Kentucky Derby. She got chills when she saw the twin spires and imagined all the history that had taken place at that very spot. They parked for a few minutes and took some pictures out front by the Barbaro statue.

When she told Macy about the racetrack, Macy vowed that she would attend the Derby in the next year or two. "Ten years of living in Kentucky, and I've never been to Churchill Downs. Can you believe that?"

Molly had told Macy about her possible plans to move to Kentucky a little more permanently, and at first her best friend was ecstatic. She was overjoyed at the thought of having Molly continue on as a roommate or be a few miles down the road at Beau's. But then she became silent, a rarity for Macy. "Are you sure about this, Moll? Don't get me wrong, I think you two are perfect for each other, but it *is* awfully soon. I'd love for you to stay, but I want to make sure you are staying for the right reasons and not because you're running from something back home."

Molly appreciated Macy's concern and candor and told her so. She definitely didn't think she was running from anything, or anyone, back home. Maybe she had been at first, but not now. She was completely over Ty and all his shenanigans, and she was looking forward to a future with Beau. While she still wasn't completely sure she was ready to move in with him, she was ready to move to Lexington, for now at least.

And nothing was permanent, she reminded herself. If things didn't work out, she could return home. And even if things did work out, Beau could always find a job back east as well. And while Molly missed her family like crazy, she had to admit that Lexington fit her like a glove. She felt more alive and free than she had in a long time, maybe ever.

The only problem was her parents and Erin; she hadn't told them of her big plans. Everyone thought she was coming home at the end of August, and Molly hadn't said anything to make them believe otherwise. They all knew about Beau, but maybe they assumed it was a summer fling, a distraction. She didn't know how she'd break the news to them that she would be home soon, but only to pack some more bags and end her lease on the carriage house. Molly could already see her mother's tears, feel her father's silence. She could almost feel

Erin's distress that her baby sister wasn't going to be a short drive away.

But it's my life, she thought. *I can live it any way I please. I'll tell everyone my plans…in just a few more days.*

~ Chapter 21 ~

As Beau made his rounds, the hospital was eerily quiet. Sure, it was night shift, but there were usually a few emergencies to keep him hopping. But not tonight.

For the countless time since she left, Beau walked past Gypsy's stall, now vacant and dark. He didn't realize how much he had fallen for the filly. She had been everyone's favorite. He had been thrilled when Molly had told him about her plans to adopt her if the owners agreed, and Beau couldn't imagine a more perfect set up. Two of his favorite girls together, a team.

Gypsy had gone back to her former life, but her path had not yet been determined. There was still a chance that her owners would decide against breeding her. Beau hoped that she was being treated like the baby doll that she was, and that her groom knew how much she liked to be scratched behind the ears and on top of her withers.

Suddenly, he felt a presence behind him and turned to see Cassidy.

"Can we talk for a minute?" She asked.

"Sure," Beau replied. "I was just getting ready to take a break. Let's go in my office," he said and led the way.

Once inside Cass turned and closed the door behind them. "Look," she said, getting straight to the point. "I just have to know. What does Molly have that I don't?" Beau could see that she was struggling to hold back tears. He instantly felt terrible. He had been too caught up in his whirlwind romance with Molly to even think about how all of this must have made Cass feel.

"Oh honey. I'm so sorry. I didn't realize how much all this might have been hurting you." He knew she had been distant over the last few weeks, but they also hadn't worked together too often either, so the situation with Cass just hadn't been at the forefront of his mind. Also, he had *thought* that she had wanted more with him, but since she had never come right out and told him, Beau assumed that her feelings weren't that serious after all.

"Just be honest with me, Beau. You said that you weren't ready to date, that you weren't over your ex, and then a few weeks later you're walking around like a lovesick puppy when some new girl comes to town. What was wrong with me? Why didn't you want *me*?" A few tears had trickled out, spilling their way onto Cassidy's cheeks. She abruptly wiped them away with the back of her hand, angry at herself for crying in front of him.

"Cass, trust me when I say there is nothing wrong with you. This wasn't a contest between you and Molly. She's not better than you in any way – she's just different. I can't describe it. I don't know what it is about her that made me fall so fast, but I just did, and I'm so very sorry if I hurt you." *This is what I get for sleeping with people from work*, Beau thought to himself.

He grabbed the box of tissues from his desk and handed them to Cass. She took one and started carefully dabbing her eyes. "I'm sorry I'm being such a baby about this, but I had to know why you chose her instead."

"Like I said, it wasn't a competition. Molly just came along at the right time. Please don't take it personally." Beau reached forward and pulled Cass into his arms and hugged her closely. He probably shouldn't have, but she seemed so heartbroken and forlorn that he wanted to comfort her. She allowed herself to be held for a short moment before breaking away. She seemed to have regained her composure.

"Sorry again about my outburst. Thanks for the clarification." She wouldn't make eye contact with him as she said this and was out the door before he could respond.

What a mess I've gotten myself into, he thought as he shook his head. Beau truly felt sorry that he had hurt Cass, but he hoped that this encounter was the end of it. She was a great girl – she just wasn't *his* girl. And she was never going to be.

Sighing quietly, Beau sat down at his desk and rested his head in his hands. On the bright side, Molly should be calling soon. She always called to say good night right before she went to bed. He knew that she had been working diligently on her new book and that she could be a night owl when she wrote. He told her not to worry about the time because he would be up. After that catastrophe, Beau just wanted to hear her voice.

As if right on cue with his thoughts, his cell rang. Beau answered without even looking at the caller ID.

"Hey darlin'. How's the book coming?" Beau asked easily.

There was a long pause on the other end before an unexpected voice answered. "Beau? Is that you?"

"Uhh…Natalie? Sorry, I thought you were someone else," Beau stammered. *Why on earth is Nat calling?* He wondered.

"No problem. Sorry to be calling so late. I figured if you weren't on night shift you'd let it go to voicemail, and I'd leave a message."

"It's okay. What can I do for you?" He asked matter-of-factly.

"Well, I'm going to be in town next week and wanted to know if I could stop by. Maybe we could grab dinner or a drink?" Natalie asked coyly.

Beau paused, unsure of how to respond. "I'm not so sure that would be a good idea. You see, I'm dating someone, and," he paused briefly, "I just can't imagine you and I would have too much to say to each other," Beau answered honestly.

"I understand Beau. I was just looking to catch up a little, that's all." Natalie went silent for a moment. "And I won't lie – I miss you. It would be nice to see a familiar face while I'm in town."

Beau was stunned. What was she saying? How could she possibly miss him when she was the one who had left?

"Nat, is everything okay?"

"Oh yes, everything's fine. I'm fine. I just, like I said, I wanted to see you." Her voice had grown quiet and sultry, and Beau could not believe what was happening.

"I really appreciate the call, but I just don't have the time right now. Have a safe trip. Take care." Beau felt bad for ending the call abruptly, but what did she expect?

Wow – that was odd, Beau thought. He wouldn't have been surprised if he never heard from Natalie again. Twice she had made her choice, and it wasn't him. But maybe he shouldn't have been so short with her. It was obvious that she wasn't as "fine" as she claimed to be, and here he was, as happy as a clam.

He realized that his harsh tone and his rush to hang up probably made him sound like a scorned lover, which he wasn't, not anymore. At that moment, Beau realized that he was completely over Nat. Sure, she had broken his heart, and sure, he had given her many years of his life, but everything had happened for the best. He and Nat had never been on the same page, had never been meant to be. He and Molly? That was a match made in heaven.

Beau decided that he wouldn't reach out to Natalie, but if she called while she was in town, and he was available, he may grab a quick drink with her. At this point, she was just an old friend, an acquaintance from a past life. And maybe Nat didn't have any ulterior motives – maybe she really did just want to catch up.

Shaking his head to himself, Beau got up to start making his rounds. *Could this night get any stranger?*

~~~~~

Molly had never completed a first draft as quickly as she had with this current novel. She attributed it to all the emotions she was feeling: sheer joy at her blissful union with Beau, absolute comfort and peace thanks to her living arrangement with her best friend, and sadness for missed opportunities with Gypsy.

She had made the mistake of going to see Gypsy at the hospital a handful of times each week so she could get to know the filly better. Not surprisingly, Molly had fallen for the special girl which made her departure back to her owners all the more painful. But for now, Molly would throw herself into the new novel, which she thought was probably going to be her best yet. She would do a thorough edit on it in the coming days and then submit the draft to her copy editor who, along with her agent, would be thrilled to be receiving it ahead of schedule.

As always, she would submit a draft to her mother as Karen loved to have a sneak peek into her daughter's work. Her mom, an avid reader and bookworm, would read through the draft multiple times offering her edits and ideas. Molly smiled as she could hear her mom's voice. "Some people are proud to have a doctor in the family, but not me. I'd rather brag about my daughter, the author."

Molly had hinted to her mom while on the phone earlier in the day that she was thinking of staying in Lexington a bit longer. "I just feel so inspired here mom. Maybe it's the change of scenery. I've never finished a draft so quickly."

"It could be the new location," her mom agreed, "but it could also be that you're in love. I've heard it in your voice for weeks now."

Her mom had told her to do whatever made her happy, but Molly knew that deep inside Karen was praying for her daughter to come home for good, and soon.

Molly had, however, told Erin the truth. Her sister had taken the news much better than she thought she would. "Ah crud. I figured Mr. Cowboy Vet would lure you away. Damn it, Moll." Erin sighed. "Well, you only live once, right? Take your time and figure it out. You don't need the answers today. Maybe you do stay in Kentucky for a few years…maybe you don't. I certainly hope that you don't, but you gotta do what's right for you."

Yes, I have to do what's right for me, Molly thought. *Beau and I will figure everything out, together.*

~ Chapter 22 ~

Beau spotted Natalie sitting at the bar. She was wearing a short, black, tight-fitting dress and matching black stilettos. By her standards, she was probably dressing down, but she clearly stuck out like a sore thumb amid the Kentucky crowd. She always had.

"Hey stranger! How are you?" Nat asked as she stood up to hug him tightly. Beau noticed that not only was she wearing his favorite perfume, but she had styled her hair the way he liked it, long and wavy. *What was she trying to do?* He wondered.

Nat had called him earlier in the day to say that she was in town, free for dinner, and would love it if he could join her. Since he was on night shift at the hospital, he knew he should have been sleeping, but figured a quick dinner after his behavior on the phone the other night was the least he could do. And besides, just in case she had any other ideas, he wanted Nat to see for herself that he was over her, that he was in love with someone else.

"You look tired. Night shift still?" She asked.

Beau nodded. "Yep. Tonight's my last night, and then I can get on a normal schedule again."

A waitress seated them at a nearby booth. Natalie carried her glass of white wine with her, and sat it on the table. Beau ordered a water and a large regular coffee. He would need the caffeine to get him through his shift, and possibly through this dinner. On second thought, maybe he should have ordered something stronger, like whiskey.

He and Nat made small talk for a bit, catching up about each other's family. Finally Nat paused and gave him a shy smile. "So, you're seeing someone, huh? What's she like?" She seemed genuinely interested.

"Her name is Molly, and she's from Maryland. She's friends with a colleague of mine. Molly is visiting for the summer, but we met completely by chance out on the trails. She's," Beau paused and smiled. "We're a lot alike."

Natalie understood and nodded. "That's something you and I never had going for us, did we? If only I could have learned to love horses. Or if only you would have moved to the west coast. Does Molly know that you'll always be married to your job?"

"Well, I wouldn't put it that way exactly, but, yes, Molly knows how much of my life is consumed by work. But she's a horse lover, so she's sympathetic. And she's a writer, so her schedule is pretty flexible."

Natalie smiled that perfect smile of hers, the one that always made his heart flip flop. He'd be lying if he said it no longer had any effect on him. It did a little. Old habits die hard. But he knew he had no future with the woman sitting across from him. She was just a pretty face.

"She sounds like a wonderful person. Maybe I'll get to meet her sometime."

Beau nodded. "Yes, maybe sometime."

~~~~~

Later that night the hospital was hopping and Beau rushed off from one emergency to another. When he had a chance to take a break, he made himself a coffee and contemplated calling Molly. He looked at the clock – it was after three in the morning. He didn't want to risk waking her up at this point. Beau missed her. His night shift had made it a little difficult to make plans since he had to sleep during the day.

Beau took another gulp of coffee, relishing its taste. He had been a coffee drinker since college and couldn't imagine a day without at least one or two cups. Beau twirled the paper cup around in his hand as he thought about Molly. He realized his arms ached to hold her.

He also wanted to tell her about his dinner with Natalie, which had gone better than expected. Nat hadn't tried any funny stuff, and while she definitely wasn't her usual perky self and was more subdued, she had seemed okay. Beau wondered if she ever regretted her decision to leave that final time, wondered if she ever thought about what their life would have been like had she stayed.

Seeing Natalie had stirred up some memories – all good ones as is normal with the passage of time. He felt no ill-will towards her now. And while he had to admit that she was just as beautiful and as elegant as ever, he had a hard time picturing himself with her. Had they really been lovers? All that seemed so foreign to him now.

As they had walked out of the restaurant, Natalie had told him that she was in town for work until the following week and was trying to get together with Peter and Angela as well. When Beau walked her to her car, Natalie had turned as if she wanted to say something but then thought the better of it.

Before Beau had a chance to contemplate that moment any longer, his beeper sounded and he was brought back to reality. Time to get to work.

~ Chapter 23 ~

Beau had a surprise waiting for him at home when he pulled up at eight o'clock the following morning. Night shift had been grueling, but he had been able to clock out on time, surprisingly. All he wanted to do was go home and sleep, but when he saw Molly sitting on his front steps, he was wide awake. There was something about that girl that just lit him up inside, zapping every nerve to life.

"I thought I'd come by and fix you a quick breakfast before you went to bed," Molly offered sweetly.

"Honey, I sure would appreciate that, but I have something else on my mind that I'd like to take care of first." Beau opened the front door with his key and then turned around to scoop Molly up in his arms. She instantly wrapped her arms around him and began kissing his neck and jaw, working her way up to his lips. By the time they made it to the bedroom, she had already thrown Beau's baseball cap to the side and was pulling off his shirt.

Beau laughed out loud. "Well someone sure is hungry for something, and I don't think it's breakfast."

Molly laughed at his joke and continued to undress Beau. "I can't help it," she whispered. "I haven't seen you in days. I've missed you."

Beau's heart melted at those words. He had longed to be with Molly, too. Being apart, if only for a few days, had been painful. As he stood up to remove his pants, he gazed down at the woman on his bed. After seeing Natalie yesterday, and thinking about their past all night, Beau was able to appreciate Molly even more. She was everything to him, and he wanted to show her.

He kneeled on the floor, leaned against the bed, and pulled Molly over towards him, spreading her legs as he did so. Molly moaned loudly as Beau bent his head and tasted her. He couldn't believe how hungry he was for her – he couldn't get enough. Molly arched her back, pushing herself into his mouth even farther while cradling his head, holding him in place by his hair. She pumped her hips until she climaxed, screaming his name as she did so.

Overcome with desire, Beau quickly pulled himself onto the bed and pushed himself inside her, and Molly wrapped her legs around his waist, drawing him closer, closer. They moved in unison until Molly climaxed a second time and Beau finished shortly thereafter, groaning softly as Molly kissed him.

Lying on the bed afterward, both were out of breath but blissfully happy. "Thank you for that," Molly said sweetly. "You were amazing."

"And you are always amazing. I was so happy to see you here when I pulled up. It's like you knew that I needed to be with you."

They caught each other up on what had happened over the last few days. Molly told him about the progress she'd made with her book and how she couldn't believe she'd finished a first draft so quickly. Beau was impressed and told her that he couldn't wait to read it. Then he told her about night shift and how busy it had been.

When Beau's cell began to ring, Molly reached over and grabbed it off the nightstand to hand to Beau. Without thinking, she looked at the front screen.

"It's…Natalie?" She said with a questioning tone as she handed the phone to Beau.

"I'll send it to voicemail," Beau said nonchalantly as he set the phone back down.

"Well, do you think it's important? You haven't talked to her in a long time, maybe something's wrong."

"I don't think so. She's in town for a few days and probably wants to get together again. We had dinner last night – just caught up a bit. She's going to see Peter and Angela too." Beau tried to downplay the fact that Natalie was in town, but immediately felt a pang of guilt for not telling Molly about the dinner yet.

"Oh I see," Molly said quietly. "Were you going to tell me that you met with her?" She tried to keep her tone in check but knew she was coming across a little accusatory. She didn't want to be the jealous girlfriend, she never had been, but she was a little worried that Beau had hidden this from her.

"Absolutely. We only went out just last night. The moment I got to the hospital, things were crazy, so I didn't have a chance to call. I'm sorry, love. I should have told you."

"So, what exactly happened?" Molly hated herself for asking that question, but her recent experience with Ty's infidelity made her a little skeptical.

Beau shook his head. "Nothing happened. I didn't particularly want to meet up, but, heck, she's not in town often. It was just two friends catching up."

"That's pretty big of you. I would hardly call any of my exes *friends*."

"Well," Beau stammered, "maybe we're not close, but she was a big part of my life for many years. She called me up and wanted to grab a drink. That was all – a drink and a quick meal." Beau reached over and ran his hand through Molly's hair. "I'm sorry if I upset you. I wasn't trying to hide anything. I would have told you last night but work was so busy."

Molly brushed Beau's hand off, stood up, and began to dress. "I know, Beau. I know it was just a misunderstanding. But I can tell you that if one of my exes came to town and wanted to get together, I would have called you and given you a heads up *before* the dinner took place. Just so you knew."

Beau shook his head in agreement. "You're right. I should have told you before. I just didn't even think about it." He paused. "But honestly, it's really not a big deal. Natalie and I are completely over and have been for quite some time."

"In the grand scheme of life, Beau, you're right. It's not a big deal. But when I find out after the fact that you and your on and off again ex – a fairly recent ex – had dinner together, it upsets me a little. Had the tables been turned, I would have had enough respect for you to tell you about it and ask if you had any objections. It's just the decent thing to do when you're in a relationship – especially a new one like ours."

Molly still couldn't believe how upset she was getting, but it hurt to think that Beau hadn't been thoughtful enough to tell her that Natalie had been in touch. If Ty had called her, she would have told Beau – just so he knew. There were no secrets – even unintentional ones.

Beau didn't know what else to say other than apologize. "Darlin', I'm truly sorry. You're right. I should have given you the chance to tell me how you felt about it before I met with her. I'm sorry."

Molly could tell that Beau was sincere and decided to drop it. "It's okay Beau," she sighed. She wanted to tell him that she wasn't normally this pushy and jealous, that the situation with Ty earlier in the year had affected her more than she had thought. She also wanted to tell him that she had overacted because she was so scared of losing him. They had only been together for a short time, yet Molly could not believe how deeply she had fallen in love. If Beau went back to his ex, which seemed like a very real possibility given their history, it would shatter her.

Instead she said, "Why don't I let you get some sleep. I'm sure you're exhausted." And she walked out.

~ Chapter 24 ~

"I think you had a perfectly normal response, especially after what Ty put you through," Macy said reassuringly.

Molly had come home, exploding through the door as if a wild herd of bulls had been chasing her. She hadn't planned to spill everything to Macy, but her friend had been at the kitchen table enjoying her morning coffee when Molly had returned. The moment Molly looked at Macy, she burst into tears.

"I know," Molly cried. "But Beau doesn't even know me that well. He probably thinks I'm some crazy, scorned lover who loses it at the drop of a hat."

Macy brought over a steaming mug of chamomile tea and handed it to Molly. "I put some honey in it, just the way you like it."

Molly gratefully accepted the mug and smiled as her best friend sat next to her on the couch. "Thank you," she said with a weak smile. "I don't know what I'd do without you."

"It's no problem at all. This is what best friends are for. But no, I'm sure he doesn't think you're some crazy, scorned lover. I would have reacted the same way. His meeting up with her caught you by surprise. You're allowed to tell him how that makes you feel," Macy reasoned.

"Mm, this is good," Molly said after she sipped her tea. "I guess you're right. I was just totally caught off guard. And I was thinking while I was driving back over here, even though this wasn't that big of a deal, it gives me pause, you know? This is someone I'm willing to uproot my entire life in Maryland for, and he can't even tell me when one of his exes is in town? Actually, I think she's his *only* ex."

"Wow – you're right. She is his only ex. That makes things tricky because Natalie's really all he's ever known." Macy agreed.

"Maybe this was a good wake up call. Maybe we're moving too fast. I can't pick up and move to Kentucky until I'm really sure that he's the one. It's just not worth it otherwise. It's too risky. And if there's the slightest chance that he'd ever consider getting back together with Natalie, then I may as well just go back to Maryland now."

Macy sighed as she listened to her friend. She wanted Molly and Beau to make it. "I think you two just need to talk again. Let Beau get some sleep, and then go grab some dinner or something. Voice your concerns and give him a chance to respond. But I agree. If you have even the tiniest of doubts about him or his intentions, don't move to Kentucky."

"Thanks Mace. I'm glad you were here so I could vent."

"Of course. Hey – why don't you come to Texas with me?" Macy was leaving the following day to visit relatives in Houston. "You can fly out with me tomorrow – stay the whole week or just a few days. Maybe a change of scenery will do you good."

Molly laughed. "I already took a trip to experience a change of scenery, remember? I came here! I'd love to go with you to Texas, but I think I'll stay here and figure everything out with Beau. Thank you for the offer though – I really appreciate it."

Macy leaned over and gave Molly a hug. "Call me if you need anything. I'll only be a short flight away!"

~~~~~

What have I done? Beau thought to himself. After Molly left he had been too worked up to go to sleep. He needed to make things right but decided to give Molly some space. Let her go home and talk everything through with Macy. He'd give her a call later in the evening, and maybe they could get something to eat and hash through this misunderstanding.

He should have told Molly about Natalie's call before he had agreed to meet up with her, but the thought never once crossed his mind. Beau knew that the get-together was completely innocent. He didn't have anything to hide. Honestly, the driving force behind him agreeing to dinner was him wanting to show Natalie that he was completely over her. That he was doing great without her. But Molly didn't know that, and the news of Natalie had blindsided her.

When he listened to the voicemail Natalie had left that morning, he was furious. She was driving up to Louisville that afternoon to see Peter and Angela and had wanted to know if he would like to join her, keep her company on the drive. Nat knew Beau was in a new relationship – what was she doing?

Beau deleted her message immediately and didn't respond. His silence would be the answer.

Before Molly, Beau would have jumped at the chance to be with Natalie again, even for something as simple as taking a drive to see some old friends. She had been his kryptonite. She had always been his weakness. But not anymore. Not since Molly.

Beau realized that he was getting drowsy again, so he decided to lie down and take a quick nap. He'd call Molly when he woke up.

When Beau stirred, he instantly knew he had slept too long as the windows were dark and the room was thick with night. The clock on the nightstand read 11:15 p.m. *Shit*, he thought as he jumped out of bed and reached for his cell. No missed calls.

He dialed Molly's number. It rang multiple times and then clicked over into her voicemail. "Hey darlin', it's me. I'm so sorry – I meant to call earlier, but I fell asleep and didn't set an alarm. If you're awake, please give me a call back, or feel free to come over. I miss you, and I'd really love to talk."

When his cell rang a few moments later, he practically tackled it thinking it was Molly. It was the hospital. "This is Beau," he answered professionally.

"Hey Beau, it's Sam, hope I didn't wake you." Sam was one of his favorite colleagues.

"Hi Sam. No, you didn't wake me. Actually I just got up from my nap – was on night shift this week."

"Ahh that means you're off tomorrow aren't you? Darn it. I was calling to see if you could cover my shift tomorrow – three to eleven. I have family visiting and they've decided to stay an extra day. But don't worry about it, didn't realize you were coming off of night shift."

Beau didn't really want to work on his day off. He wanted to spend time with Molly and make sure things were okay between them, but Sam had covered many shifts for Beau and was a good friend to have at the hospital. Of course he'd help him out. "It's no problem at all, Sam. I don't have any plans tomorrow, so I'll cover for you."

When Beau hung up he thought about calling Molly again, but if she had been up, or had wanted to talk, she would've called.

~ Chapter 25 ~

Molly had been asleep by the time that Beau had called the previous night. The day's events had exhausted her, so she had turned in earlier than normal. She called him after she had breakfast but his phone must have been off because it went straight to voicemail. She didn't leave a message.

Deciding that a ride through the countryside was what she needed, she hopped in the car and headed over to see Hunter. After she tacked up her favorite boy, they hit the trails, now familiar to Molly, and she thought about how funny life could be, how quickly it could change. While she felt better about everything that had happened, she was sad that the honeymoon period of the relationship appeared to be over.

"Well, I guess it wasn't so bad for our first fight," Molly said aloud to Hunter who flicked his ears back, acknowledging the conversation. "I guess it was wrong of me to think that Beau was perfect. No one is and it was unfair of me to hold him to such high standards. Hopefully we can catch up today."

As they looped around the trail and were headed back to the barn, Molly loosened the reins and let Hunter drop his head and stretch out. It was times like this that Molly thanked her lucky stars that horses were a part of her life, and thought about how blessed she was to have been born into a horse-loving family. Even though she wasn't particularly upset at Beau anymore, she relished her ability to hop on the back of a horse and get away from it all for a bit. Horses were the ultimate outlet for stress relief, and she knew for certain with every fiber of her being that she could never live without this magnificent animal.

Horses had been her one constant. They defined her. That very thought made her yearn for Gypsy, and she made a mental note to follow up with her owners to see if they had changed their minds. She just had to have that filly, and she knew that persistence paid off. As her mother always said, "the squeaky wheel gets the grease." *I'll call every day if it means getting Gypsy*, Molly thought.

~~~~~

It was around noon when Beau woke up from yet another nap. He had stayed up most of the night reading, but had apparently dozed off sometime in the early morning hours. *Night shift really takes its toll*, he thought.

When he reached for his cell, he realized the battery was dead. He quickly stuck his phone into its charger, waited a minute for it to boot up, and then called Molly. Again it rang and went to voicemail. "Hey, it's me again. I forgot to charge my phone last night, and the battery died. Sorry if I missed your call. Anyway, you're probably out riding on this beautiful day, and I, unfortunately, am headed back into work at three, told a friend I'd cover his shift. I really hope to hear from you soon though. Feel free to stop by the hospital if you'd like. I love you, Molly, don't forget that."

Beau sincerely hoped that Molly was out riding or running errands and wasn't deliberately avoiding his call.

When he arrived at the hospital, Cassidy was already there and brought him up to speed on some new patients. Two emergency colic surgeries had taken place the night before, and Beau was pleased to see that both horses were slated to make full recoveries.

He was also relieved to see that Cassidy seemed almost back to her normal self. She had been short with him since she confronted him last week, but today Cass seemed fairly content as she made rounds with him. Beau prayed things would stay this way.

The rest of the afternoon flew by, but in the early evening, Beau received an unexpected visitor. Walking in as if she owned the place was Natalie, dressed to impress and chatting delightfully with Cassidy. They both looked up as he approached.

Beau cleared his throat. "Natalie, can I help you?"

"Hey Beau, thanks for returning my call yesterday," she said sarcastically with that Cheshire cat smile of hers. "I had a great time with Pete and Ang – we would have loved it if you had joined."

"Can I help you?" Beau asked bluntly. He didn't appreciate Natalie showing up at his work without warning. He was sure his tone conveyed this message as Cassidy's eyebrows shot up, and then she mumbled something about "making rounds" and turned the corner, making herself scarce.

Natalie looked him straight in the eye for a moment without speaking. Then, quietly, her voice barely above a whisper, she asked if there was some place they could go to talk in private.

Beau was tempted to tell her no and ask her to leave immediately. But he knew what Natalie was capable of when she didn't get her way and didn't want her to make a scene, so he told her to follow him back into his office where he left the door mostly ajar.

"Why are you here, Nat?" He asked.

With a sudden rush of words and tears, Natalie told Beau that she wanted him back, that she was still in love with him, that she had made a mistake, again. She hadn't come into town for work but rather to win him back. If he would just give her one final chance, he wouldn't regret it, she pleaded.

"I promise we'll make it work this time," Natalie said with tears streaming down her cheeks. "Let's get married, Beau. Right now. Today."

Beau couldn't believe what he was hearing. Even though Natalie had come back to him before, he hadn't expected her to return a second time and with a marriage proposal at that. As he stood there watching his beautiful ex-girlfriend sob, he was struck by the fact that he felt nothing for her. In the months following their second break up, he had prayed fervently for this moment, that she'd come to her senses and return. But now that it was actually happening, he was shocked at the numbness he felt.

He let Natalie say her piece, handing her a tissue to stop the steady flow of tears. Once she had calmed down and regained her composure, he gently told her that it was over, and that he was in love with someone else. He appreciated her honesty and the effort she made to come to Kentucky, but it wasn't going to be like last time when he had quickly taken her back with no questions asked. They were done.

Natalie accepted her fate quietly, somehow sensing that nothing she said would change Beau's mind. She nodded to herself, and told him that she would have regretted not making one final attempt. When she had dried her eyes, she took a deep breath, walked over to Beau, and wrapped her arms around him. She held him tight, and whispered in his ear, "I hope Molly knows just how lucky she is." Then she took his face in her hands and kissed him directly on the lips.

And just like she had twice before, Natalie turned on her heel and was gone. He heard her murmur goodbye to Cassidy, who had just passed her in the hall, but she kept on walking and didn't look back.

~ Chapter 26 ~

"Dang it, Hunter. I missed Beau's call again," Molly said to the horse when she returned back from her ride. Not wanting to drop her phone and break it, she usually left it in her car or in Hunter's tack trunk where it would be safe.

After listening to his voicemail, she decided that she would go home, shower and change, pick up some dinner, and meet him at the hospital. Hopefully Beau would be able to take a quick break for some food.

Satisfied with her plans for the evening, Molly hummed softly to herself as she clipped Hunter in cross-ties in the wash stall and hosed him off. She then poured shampoo along his back and curried it in with her wash mitt, creating lots of bubbles. Hunter, enjoying the full body massage, flapped his lips together, a sign of contentment and appreciation. Molly laughed, and thought to herself that maybe everything was going to be okay after all.

~~~~~

Beau felt mentally exhausted after Natalie left, and he was still in disbelief. Had she really come back a second time? While it had been hard to stand there and watch her cry, he knew he had made the right decision. That chapter of his life was officially closed.

After fixing himself another cup of coffee, Beau went back to his desk and sat down. As if on cue, his cell phone rang, interrupting his thoughts. Hoping it was Molly, he grabbed it quickly. It was his sister.

"Hey Annie – how are you?"

Crying hysterically, Annie told him that their father had had another heart attack. "He's being rushed into surgery now, but it's not looking good. They're telling mom she needs to prepare herself." She dissolved into fits of choking sobs. Michael, her husband, took the phone from her. "Hey Beau, it's Mike. You may want to get here as quick as you can," he said grimly.

Beau grabbed his truck keys and sprinted out of the hospital as if he were on fire. He'd call his supervisor on his way to the airport and explain his absence.

~~~~~

Molly, dressed in jeans, a casual top, and flip flops, walked out of Beau's favorite Mexican restaurant carrying two huge bags of take-out. They both loved Mexican food, so she had ordered chips, salsa, and guacamole, quesadillas, enchiladas for herself, and a large burrito for Beau. She was looking forward to talking with him and hoped he would have time for dinner with her.

Even though she had seen him the day before, it felt like forever. They were playing phone tag, which seemed almost impossible to do in this day and age, so she figured surprising him at the hospital would be the best way to ensure she actually got to speak with him.

Once in the hospital, she walked up to the receptionist's desk and asked to see Beau at the same time Cassidy walked by. "Oh, he's not here," Cassidy replied before the receptionist could answer.

"Oh I thought he said he was covering a shift this evening for another colleague," Molly said.

Cass nodded. "He was, but I saw him sprinting out of here about a half hour ago."

Molly thought that seemed odd. "Did he say where he was going?"

Cassidy paused for a moment, unsure of what to tell Molly. Her supervisor had just told her that Beau had a family emergency in Georgia, but clearly Molly didn't know that yet. Cassidy saw her chance, and took it.

When the receptionist had turned away, Cassidy walked closer to Molly and whispered in her ear. "He didn't, but all I know is that his ex showed up, and she wanted to talk. I left to give them some privacy, but walked by later and heard her crying in his office, begging him to take her back. I was on my way to see a patient, so I didn't hear more, but when I walked by a second time, I saw her kiss him. A few minutes later, I saw him running out of here like he was being chased by wild dogs. My guess is that he ran after her."

Molly felt like she had been punched in the stomach. She didn't know how to respond other than to question Cassidy. "Are you sure it was Natalie? Couldn't he have been running out for an emergency call?"

"It was definitely her. She introduced herself to me when she arrived, and I talked with her until Beau came by. And it wouldn't have been an emergency either. Anything like that would have come into the hospital, and we'd have record of it. Our doctors don't leave."

Molly looked absolutely devastated, and for a moment Cassidy almost came out and told her the truth. She had overheard Natalie begging Beau to take her back, but she also heard him telling her that it was over for good. And yes, she did see Natalie kiss him briefly, but it was right before she turned and walked out.

Cassidy didn't want to lie, but Molly had ruined her chances of being with Beau, and Cassidy didn't like when things didn't go her way. Had Molly not come along when she did, Cass was sure she eventually would have won Beau over.

Clearly understanding the situation now, Molly took a deep breath and sighed. Beau had made his choice. Natalie had come to him again and professed her love, and he had chased after her to accept it. She knew where she stood. "Are you two hungry?" She asked Cassidy and the receptionist. "Have some dinner." She dropped the bags on the desk and left without another word.

~~~~~~

Luckily, Beau was able to get a flight immediately out of Lexington and made it to Georgia in record time. He hadn't even stopped home to pack a bag, just raced to the airport and booked the first flight he could catch.

When his plane landed, he checked his messages and had a text from his brother. "Dad's out of surgery. Still touch and go but he's holding his own." Beau prayed ardently that his dad would pull through. He knew he should have come down the previous month when he had that scare with the chest pain. *Why haven't I visited more?* He thought, punishing himself for working too hard and not making enough time to be with his family.

The cab ride from the airport to the hospital seemed to take forever, and when the driver pulled up in front, Beau threw some cash at him, jumped out, and sprinted away before the car had fully come to a complete stop.

A receptionist directed him to the cardiac ICU, and he ran through the halls like a kid late for class. He found his entire family gathered in the waiting room just outside the ICU. Everyone looked exhausted with red-rimmed eyes and wrinkled clothes that had clearly been slept in. It was just after midnight.

His mother jumped up when she saw her youngest son and flung her arms around him. "Oh Beau, I'm so glad you're here," she said in between her tears. "He's trying to hang on. The doctors said the first twenty-four hours are the hardest, and that he's seen cases like your dad's go either way."

Beau held his mother tight. "He's a fighter, mama, you know that. He won't give up."

~ Chapter 27 ~

The next morning, Molly woke up on a mission. It was time to take control of her life.

Thankfully, Macy had already left for her trip by the time Molly returned home the previous night. She had met up with her mom, brother, and sister-in-law in Texas for a visit with her extended relatives, so Molly was grateful that she didn't have to explain why her eyes were so puffy and red. She would tell Macy about everything, but not right now.

She dressed quickly, hopped in her car, and typed the address for Dawson Estate into her phone. She was tired of waiting for people to make up their minds.

Down Pisgah Pike she sped and when she got to Old Frankfort Pike, she made a right. Two more miles down the road, a left hand turn, and she was there. Of course she was met with a grand gated entrance, but she leapt out of her car, kept it running, and hit a button on the call box.

"Can I help you?" A voice came through the tiny box.

"Yes…hi…my name is Molly Sorrenson, and I'm here to speak with the Dawsons about one of their horses I'd like to purchase. I don't have an appointment, but I won't take much of their time."

"Hold please," the box said.

Molly's adrenaline was pumping. When she had decided the night before that she was going to make a final offer on Gypsy, she hadn't thought the entire plan through. Now that she was actually here, she was nervous.

The box was still silent. She assumed the secretary was checking with the Dawsons or maybe their personal assistant, to see what to do about this crazy woman at their front gate. Molly was so anxious that she was shaking, but she wasn't going to leave until she had talked to someone about Gypsy. Enough was enough.

The box came back to life. "Miss, please drive down to the training barn. It's the second driveway on your right. Marcus, the assistant trainer, will meet you."

Molly was virtually speechless. "Thank you," she blurted out before dashing back to her car. The gates were opening.

The driveway was miles long with large maples lining both sides. Beyond the trees on either side were large fields with four-board fencing painted black. It was one of the most beautiful places Molly had ever seen. It was like something out of a movie.

When she made the second right and wound her way up to the barn, she saw a man standing out front with his arms crossed.

Oh please let this go well, she prayed.

She got out of her car and plastered on her biggest smile. "Hi, my name is Molly Sorrenson, and I'm here to inquire about one of the Dawsons' fillies."

The man stepped forward and offered his hand. "My name's Marcus. The Dawsons aren't home right now, but I've been instructed to speak with you," he said very matter-of-factly.

Molly couldn't quite get a read on this man, but he seemed nice enough even though he had crossed his arms again and wasn't quick to smile. "Oh thank you. I really appreciate your time. And I won't take much of it. I've come to make an offer on Gypsy, the two year old filly who was recently at Rood and Riddle Hospital with the bowed tendon."

At that moment, Gypsy, who was stabled about five stalls down inside the barn, hung her head over and whinnied in Molly's direction. "Hey Gyps! There's my girl," Molly called, acknowledging the sweet horse. "Have the Dawsons made a decision on whether or not they're going to keep her as a broodmare?"

"I don't think they have," Marcus answered honestly. "I'll call you when they make their decision."

Molly was flustered. "Actually, Marcus, I'm leaving town to head home today, going back to Maryland, and I really want to take Gypsy with me. Is there any way I could speak with the Dawsons? You see," she looked at him pleadingly, "I just really must have this horse, and I'm prepared to make a fair offer based on her pedigree and training thus far." When Marcus hesitated, Molly went on. "I'm sorry, Marcus. I don't mean to put you in an awkward position, but I can't leave until I have an answer."

She could tell that Marcus wasn't really sure what to do with her, but he told her that he'd see if he could get Mr. Dawson on the phone and ask him. "He won't be happy to have his vacation interrupted, but since you're leaving today, I can see why you'd like an answer."

He walked down the aisle into the office, and Molly went over to Gypsy and threw her arms around her neck. "Oh I've missed you girl! How have you been?" She asked as she played with the beautiful horse's mane. She looked the picture of health.

A few minutes later Marcus returned. "Looks like you're in luck. They said you can have her for two thousand dollars. With her bloodlines, she's worth much more, but they've decided to let her go and want her to have a nice home."

"Really?" Molly cried. "I can't believe it! Thank you so much!" She threw herself at Marcus, giving him a big hug. "I really appreciate your help!" Marcus, obviously embarrassed, turned a deep shade of red and looked uncomfortable, but there was a smile on his face.

"It was no trouble at all," he muttered.

Molly then turned to Gypsy and hugged her as well. "Did you hear that girl? You're going home with me. You're going to be mine," she said softly as she stroked her silky neck. A few tears streamed down Molly's face, but she didn't care. Gypsy was coming home with her. She'd think about the rest later.

She followed Marcus back to the office where she wrote a check and signed a few papers acknowledging the transfer of ownership. He gave her all of Gypsy's records, quite a few from her extended stay in the hospital. Then he helped her find a reputable shipper who could van Gypsy from Kentucky to Maryland.

About an hour later everything was good to go. Molly would be leaving for Maryland later that day, and Gypsy would follow two days later.

Molly planted one final kiss on Gypsy's nose, and told her that she'd see her in just two short days. "Be a good girl for the shipper, okay? I want you home safe and sound." She turned and gave Marcus another hug. "Really, Marcus," she said with tears threatening to spill over again, "I can't thank you enough. And please give my gratitude to the Dawsons. They've made me the happiest girl in the world."

~ Chapter 28 ~

Beau paid the cashier in the hospital cafeteria for his large coffee and bagel with cream cheese. He pocketed the change and stopped at the counter behind her and grabbed three mini creamers and a plastic knife to spread the cream cheese. He settled in at a small table next to a window.

Not long after Beau had arrived, he was able to go into the ICU to see his dad. He sat next to him for his allotted fifteen minutes, held his father's hand, and talked to him even though his father was not alert. "Keep fighting, dad. I know you can do it. We all love you so much." Beau's eyes started to tear up just thinking about what his dad was going through.

Around five o'clock in the morning, Tate came back to the hospital with a change of clothes for Beau, who was still in his work scrubs. It was about six-thirty when Beau realized he was starving.

They had one scare during the night when his father's blood pressure dropped, but other than that, he was hanging in there. The doctor had come by right before Beau had gone for something to eat and told them that if his dad continued to hold his own throughout the day, he'd be cautiously optimistic that he'd make a full recovery. Beau prayed that this would be true.

A few hours later, after taking his turn to sit with his father again, Beau walked out of the hospital to call Molly. In his haste to get to Georgia he had completely forgotten to check in with her. *Was our fight really the last time I spoke with her?* Beau wondered.

He was about to dial Molly's number when Tate walked out, so Beau hung up quickly. "Any news?" He hurriedly asked his older brother.

"No news. Just thought I'd come out here for some fresh air. I see you had the same idea."

"I can't believe this happened. Dad had been doing so well, right? Mom assured me he had been taking care of himself, taking his medication, eating well." Beau shook his head.

"It's true," replied Tate. "He was doing everything right, looked like the picture of health. They chalked up that scare last month to just some heartburn, but now they're not so sure."

Beau sighed. "I hate being so far away. Sometimes I think I ought to pack up my bags and just come home. Be with my family."

Tate looked at his kid brother and smiled. "Don't feel guilty, Beau. You have an amazing career in Kentucky. You can't be everything to everyone. Maybe one day you'll come home, but in the meantime, don't sweat it. Annie and I, and Belle and Mike, we have everything under control."

"Oh I know you do. Y'all are wonderful, but I should be around to help."

"But you are. You're here now, and that's all that matters." Tate put a hand on his brother's shoulder. "And you call mama more than any of us do, and we all live right down the street. She reminds us of that quite frequently," Tate said with a laugh. "And besides, I hear you have yourself a pretty little lady back in Kentucky. Tell me about her."

"Well, she's actually from Maryland, and is visiting her friend, who's a colleague of mine, for the summer. Her name's Molly, and she couldn't be more different from Natalie."

Tate laughed at that one. He knew the whole story with Natalie and always wondered what Beau had seen in someone who was so polar opposite from him in every way. "So you're saying that you and Molly are two peas in a pod, huh? And I bet she likes horses."

Beau smiled at his brother. "She loves them. Molly's just a wonderful, caring, genuine person. And she's so beautiful."

"So what are you guys gonna do?" Tate asked. "Is she going to stay in Kentucky, or is she headed back to Maryland at the end of the summer?"

Beau looked out over the parking lot and admitted to himself that he had been wondering the same thing lately. The fact that he and Molly hadn't been able to talk since their fight didn't sit too well with him. "I'm not exactly sure," he answered Tate. "The plan was for her to stay in Kentucky for a bit, maybe even move in with me. But we had a little misunderstanding just before I left to come here, and I haven't been able to connect with her since."

Tate looked at Beau thoughtfully. "I'm sure you guys will work it out. If she's been around you for more than two minutes, then she ought to know that you don't have a mean bone in your entire body. She'll come around."

Beau sighed again. "I sure hope so." He knew he had to get in touch with Molly soon and make sure everything was okay, but all he could think about right now was his dad.

A few moments later Mike came running out of the doors. "Your father's awake!" He shouted. He was grinning from ear to ear.

Beau and Tate quickly raced back into the hospital, following closely behind Mike. They found the rest of their family crowded around their father's bed in the ICU, more than exceeding the two person per bedside limit. But they didn't care – their father had come back to them.

Beau's mother was kneeling by her husband's side, holding his left hand in both of hers, tears flowing freely down her cheeks. His dad, still too weak to talk, looked back at her and nodded, letting her know that everything was going to be okay. Then he turned and looked at his kids and their spouses and gave an easy grin.

With his head bowed and his eyes closed, Beau said a quick prayer thanking God for seeing his father safely through yet another trial.

~ Chapter 29 ~

Giddy as a school girl, Molly turned out of the driveway of Dawson Estate and almost laughed out loud. She could not believe she had marched onto their property and practically demanded that they part with Gypsy. But it had worked! She had signed the papers officially turning ownership over to her, and she couldn't be happier.

Of course, she was heartbroken about Beau, but she told herself she'd think about him later. She knew she would cry over him on the long drive home to Maryland, but for now she needed to stay strong and run a few more errands.

Next on the agenda was to swing by Fairfield Farm and say goodbye to Hunter. Molly was truly going to miss that sweet old guy. He had been a perfect summer horse for her Back to Basics trip, and she had enjoyed their hacks through the countryside, as well as their dressage lessons with Barb.

She drove up the long drive and parked next to the stable. Hunter had been turned out in the paddock just off to the right, so Molly ran inside and grabbed a fistful of treats from his bucket, walked out to the fence, and called for Hunter. Recognizing her voice and his name, his head shot up instantly. "Come on you sweet boy!" Molly shouted and Hunter took off toward her, effortlessly cantering over to his friend.

He stood politely at the fence with Molly while she fed him treats and patted his neck. She praised him lavishly and told him how wonderful he was, how much she had appreciated his companionship over the summer.

"You be a good boy for your mom, okay? I'm going to miss you so much." At that, Molly felt a lump in her throat and had difficulty swallowing. Her eyes welled up with tears. She was going to miss this big guy. Hunter, she realized, had represented a respite from all the pain she had brought with her from Maryland. He had become her safety, easing her away from her recent past while helping her remember another one, a past filled with horses and love and wonderful memories. Hunter had rekindled her excitement for training, and it was because of him that she had decided she was definitely ready for another horse.

And it was while riding him that she had met Beau. Molly sighed as she hugged the horse hard. She'd think about that later. Right now, she just wanted to be with Hunter.

The horse stood patiently with Molly for another twenty minutes while she fawned over him and fed him handfuls of grass she plucked from the other side of the fence. But only too soon she realized it was time to leave. She planted one last kiss on Hunter's nose, and promised to return again to see him soon. "I love you boy…and thank you for everything."

As Molly walked back to her car, she was overcome by her emotions and tears streamed down her face. She wiped them quickly, hoping she wouldn't run into any of the other boarders. She turned around one last time and waved to Hunter, who was still standing at the fence, watching her.

She took a few deep breaths when she got in her car, buckled up, and pulled herself together. She still had to go back to Macy's and pack the rest of her clothes as quickly as possible if she was going to get on the road at a reasonable hour today.

Back at Macy's, it didn't take her long to gather her belongings. Within a half hour, her suitcases were packed and loaded into her Explorer. She thought about leaving Macy a note, but decided against it. Her friend was on vacation until the following week. Molly would call before Macy got home and explain the situation over the phone. She knew her friend would be devastated that she'd left without saying goodbye in person, but she knew Macy would understand that Molly did what she felt she had to do.

Molly grabbed two water bottles out of the fridge, threw a few snacks in a bag, and then looked around one last time. Despite a heart-wrenching, abrupt ending, she had had a wonderful trip and she would never regret coming to Kentucky and spending some quality time with her best friend.

After she shut and locked the door behind her, Molly took her key off its ring and pushed it back through the mail slot.

~~~~~

She made good time heading east on I-64 out of Lexington. Sadly, even though the views on both sides of the road were magnificent, Molly couldn't get out of the area fast enough.   Everywhere she looked reminded her of Beau and the promise of their future together. Was it really just a few short days ago that she was willing to call Lexington *home*?

As soon as she crossed over the West Virginia state line she exhaled deeply and realized that she had been practically holding her breath during her drive through Kentucky. She wanted to put as much room between her and Beau as possible. *Although*, she thought, *who knows where he is? He and Natalie could have gone to California for all I know.*

But now Molly was out. She was free again. She was in control of her life and her destiny, and she didn't need anyone else. Molly would be fine by herself, as she always was.

She saw a sign for a Pilot gas station and took the next exit. As her car was filling up, she went inside and made herself a large cup of coffee. The clerk at the counter who rung her up complimented the Baltimore Orioles shirt Molly was wearing. "Thank you," she replied with a smile. "It's an old favorite."

As soon as she got back on the road, she checked her phone that doubled as her GPS. She was still many hours from home, and sadly, she realized, she was already a few hours from Lexington, from Macy, from Hunter, and from Beau, if he was still in town.

When the tears that she had been holding back came pouring down, Molly didn't even try to stop them. When Cassidy had told her that Beau had run out after Natalie, Molly had been completely shocked. While she didn't deny what Cassidy was saying, it didn't truly register that he was gone, and that they would never be together again.

She thought about how she had walked out of the hospital with her head held as high as she could manage under the circumstances, and how she had sat in her car for quite some time just thinking about what she should do next. Should she call him? No, he had made his choice. Should she call Macy? No, Molly didn't want to interrupt her well-deserved vacation with her family. Then it hit her – she should go home. *But not without my horse.*

Molly had driven back to the apartment and packed some of her things. Then she had looked up the address to Dawson Estate online and jotted it down on a piece of paper. Her stomach growled as she did so, and she immediately regretted leaving all that wonderful Mexican food behind at the hospital. She fixed herself a bowl of cereal, and then went to bed.

When Molly awoke on her mission, she realized that she had been fueled by anger, her shock fading away into a controlled rage that had given her the courage to march onto the grounds of the Dawsons' and ask for Gypsy.

And now, just a few short hours later on the car ride back to Maryland, she was sobbing. Beau was gone. He had chosen a jagged past over a bright future with her, and Molly was heartbroken. Had she really let herself believe that he was the one? Was it just last week that she had been preparing to tell her family that she was moving to Lexington for good?

Sobs racked Molly's body, and she had to pull over at the next exit. She sat and cried with her face buried in her hands for quite some time. When she stopped and took a deep breath, she realized that she had never cried like this over Ty. She had felt sadness at his infidelity and depression over the loss of someone she had trusted, but she had never felt devastated. Molly had given her heart to Beau, totally and completely, and he had crushed it.

A full half hour passed before Molly was calm enough to drive again. When she eased her SUV back onto the highway, the tears were still flowing, but she was no longer hysterical and shaking.

She drove for more than an hour before she finally stopped crying. Her eyes felt like they were on fire, dry and prickly. As she closed them briefly to try and give them a moment's relief, her phone rang. It was her mom. *May as well get this over with*, Molly thought.

"Hey mom," Molly answered.

There was a pause. "Moll? What's wrong?" Her mother asked. "I can tell you've been crying."

"Yeah mom, I was. Look, it's a really long story, and I'll fill you in later, but the good news is that I'm coming home…today. I'm in West Virginia right now."

"What? Molly, are you serious? Molly, tell me what happened. Is it Beau?"

Molly sighed. "Yes, it's Beau," she said with her voice quivering. "But please, can we talk about it later? And I need you to do me a favor anyway. Could you go to the barn and get a stall ready for me? I got a new horse. She'll be home the day after tomorrow." Molly smiled at the thought of seeing her sweet new girl again.

"Wow, you're just full of surprises today. Of course, I'll prepare a stall immediately. When will *you* be home?"

"The GPS says I should be home around ten tonight. I'm going to be exhausted, so I'll go straight to the carriage house. I'll be over tomorrow to see you though. Does that work?" Molly prayed that her mother would give her some space tonight.

Her mom sighed into the phone. "Yes, that's fine. I'd love to see you tonight, honey, but tomorrow works. You be careful driving, and then get some sleep tonight. Call or text me when you get home."

"I will mom. And can you tell dad and Erin? I just don't feel much like talking right now."

"Of course. Be safe Molly. I love you."

"I love you, too."

Molly ended the call and sighed. *So glad that's over*, she thought gratefully. She was surprised that she had kept her composure. Thank goodness her mother hadn't pried, or Molly would have lost it and started bawling all over again.

Three hours later Molly smiled to herself when she crossed the Maryland state line. West Virginia was such a tough drive with all its mountains and valleys and curves. But Molly had made it, and she was back where she belonged. *Maryland, my Maryland*, her home.

Molly decided that she'd give Macy a call this evening after all. She didn't want to put a damper on her vacation, but she didn't want Macy to come home to an empty apartment without some explanation either.

But it was official, Molly's Back to Basics trip was over, and it was back to reality. She was sure she'd fall back into her old routine fairly quickly. And she had something else to look forward to – Gypsy. Molly would have her local vet out to give the new horse a quick exam, and then Molly would develop a training plan. She couldn't wait to get into the saddle and ride Gypsy across Maryland's scenic hunt country.

And then there was Molly's latest book which had been sent to her copyeditor and agent. She'd follow up with them to see what their first impressions were. But in the meantime, Molly had come up with the perfect title. It was simple, yet provided the reader with enough description. She'd call it, *Lexington: A Novel*.

~ Chapter 30 ~

It was dark by the time Molly took the exit from I-695 onto I-83 north. She stopped briefly in Deep Creek Lake again for a quick bite to eat, and then made good time traveling through Maryland's westernmost counties.

She stayed on I-83 for just a few miles before taking the exit for Shawan Road in Hunt Valley. Even though she wasn't returning home under the best circumstances, she had to admit that she had missed this area. It was funny, Molly mused to herself, how much she had looked forward to her trip to Lexington. She hadn't been able to get out of town fast enough, and now she was actually glad to be home.

East on Shawan Road led her to York Road, onto which she made a left, heading away from the congestion of the business parks and shopping centers and into pure horse country. A few more miles and she'd be turning into the separate drive that wound around the barn and directly to the carriage house.

The full moon lit miles and miles of horse fence. True, none of the farms in the area were as glamorous as the ones she had passed daily in Kentucky, but they didn't have to be top of the line. The owners of these farms viewed their horses as family and their sport as a hobby, not a business. Most of these were the homes of eventers and foxhunters and trail riders. *How could I have seriously thought of leaving this place?* Molly thought wistfully to herself. This was her own little paradise.

Macy had echoed similar sentiments when they had spoken on the phone about two hours prior. Molly had hated to interrupt Macy's vacation with bad news, but her best friend deserved to know what was going on.

"I just can't believe it, Molly, I really can't. Beau and I didn't talk about it much, but he had mentioned Natalie a few times, and he always said he'd had enough of her," Macy explained.

"I know. He seemed truly genuine when he said they were over, that their dinner had meant nothing. He said it was just two friends catching up," Molly responded.

"Well, you didn't have to pack up and rush out just because he turned out to be a cad," Macy said, "but I can understand your need to put as much space as possible in between you and the situation. And honestly, Moll, Maryland is wonderful. You have everyone there except for me. You couldn't ask for a better home, a better life."

Molly smiled to herself. "Thanks Mace. I know – I'm still a lucky girl, despite being pretty unlucky in love recently. And Gypsy's coming, too! She'll be home in two days."

"See? You have so many wonderful things to look forward to. Training your new horse, which, by the way, I am super jealous about. Gypsy is a star in her own right already. I can't wait to see what you two accomplish together. And your new book! It will be out early next year, right?" As always, Macy's enthusiasm was infectious. She could make the best of any situation.

"Yes, it will be out in January or February; although, if the editing process moves faster than usual, it might be out by Christmas."

Molly could hear Macy smile through the phone. "Ahh, my best friend, the famous writer. I'm so proud of all you've done."

Molly felt her voice catch in her throat. "I miss you already, Mace. Thanks for a wonderful summer. Your hospitality, your generosity – it really meant a lot. I love you."

Macy laughed softly on the other end of the line. "You are such a softie, you know that? But I love you, too. This has been one of the best summers ever, thanks to you."

Molly knew that living alone again was going to be an adjustment. She had enjoyed talking with Macy at the end of the day, recounting what she'd done, where she'd gone, the latest and greatest with Beau or her riding. And she had liked hearing about Macy's work at the hospital, about the various cases and her friend's thoughts on each. Molly was definitely going to be lonely, but she'd combat that by filling her days with Gypsy and numerous calls and texts to Macy and Erin.

When she pulled up in front of her little house, she was happy to see that the outside light was on. Her mother texted that she would run over that evening to open up the house a bit and drop off some necessities like milk and cereal. Her mom knew her too well.

She unlocked the front door and stepped inside, and Molly was both relieved and disappointed to see that everything was exactly the same.

She attributed her mixed emotions to the fact that, no matter what, home always had a way of making her feel better, but she hadn't expected to return home with such a dark cloud hanging over her head. The distance would help, she told herself. It's not like she'd run into Beau at the feed store or at the local pub. For that, she was grateful.

And who knew where Beau even was. Did he return to Los Angeles with Natalie? Was she moving to Lexington for him? Molly felt tears well up in her eyes as she thought about their reunion, about Beau wrapping his arms around Natalie, arms that had been wrapped tightly around her not so long ago, around his first and, quite possibly, only love. *Had I even meant anything to him?* Molly wondered sadly.

She shook her head as if trying to clear all of the painful thoughts and decided to get to work unpacking. Just like after her break up with Ty, Molly needed to stay busy. With Ty it had been so easy. She was finishing up her latest novel and was able to throw herself at it with an intensity she didn't know she'd possessed. But she didn't need her writing this time. She had Gypsy now.

Her heart skipped a beat as she thought about her new filly. She prayed that she'd have a safe journey from Kentucky. Those mountains in West Virginia were nothing to sneeze at, and she hoped the driver would take his time.

But the thought of a new horse truly made her giddy. Her mom had already prepared a stall for her at their farm, and Molly would go over to check out everything and wait for the new arrival.

Just like Macy had said, Molly was going to have a bright future with Gypsy. *Everything is going to be okay*, she silently reminded herself, nodding her head. She just needed to take it one day at a time.

Molly laughed to herself when she saw a package of Bergers Cookies on the kitchen table with a handwritten note from her mother. *Figured you had missed these.* She sure had, and she could definitely use one of them right now. The cookies were native to

Baltimore, and Molly had grown up eating the rich dessert. It was funny, she thought to herself as she stared at the simple packaging. No one called them Bergers Cookies; everyone in the area called them *Berger* Cookies, dropping the 's.'

With a large glass of milk, Molly sat down at the table and indulged in two cookies, and with their incredibly thick fudgy icing, that was about all she could eat at one time. The actual cookie itself was very plain, but was slathered in thick, chocolate icing, making it a decadent treat.

Molly toyed with the package of cookies and smiled slightly. Gypsy and Berger Cookies. What more did a girl need?

~ Chapter 31 ~

Beau was utterly exhausted when he finally arrived home in Kentucky two days later. His dad was doing much better, and the doctors were very pleased with his daily improvements. Beau had a nice conversation with his dad not too long before Beau had to go to the airport and catch his plane back.

"Thanks for coming, son. I heard you went straight from work to the airport and didn't even stop home to pack a bag. That wasn't necessary. I wasn't going anywhere." His dad's eyes twinkled.

"I know that dad, but I didn't want to waste any time. Besides, Tate and I are basically the same size. It was like old times again with me gettin' my big brother's hand-me-downs," Beau said with a grin.

His father laughed gently while holding a pillow firmly to his chest. "Well, don't you go worrying about me none. The docs say I'm gettin' out of here in a few days."

"Yeah, that's what I heard too. I know mama will be glad to have you home again."

Beau's dad looked at his son thoughtfully. "Say, how's that little lady your mama's been goin' on about? Molly, right?"

Beau paused. "Well dad, I think she's okay. I haven't been able to get a hold of Molly since I came down here. I called when I first arrived, but she didn't answer. Then my phone died, and of course I didn't bring my charger." He had asked Tate to bring his charger to the hospital, but with everything that had happened, it had completely slipped his brother's mind. "I'm going swing by her place when I get home tonight."

"That sounds like a good idea," his dad said. "And don't come down here again without her. Your mama and I would really like to meet her."

Beau smiled. "You bet dad."

It was almost nine o'clock that night when Beau pulled up in front of Macy's apartment complex. He rang the bell of her apartment and waited. No answer. Then he turned around and scanned the parking area and realized that neither Molly's nor Macy's cars were there. Where could they be?

Then he remembered that Macy was on vacation with her family, so her car was probably at the airport. *So where is Molly?*

Beau got back into his truck and shut the door behind him. Figuring that he had nowhere else to be, he leaned his seat back and decided to wait for a bit in hopes that Molly would return soon. Within two minutes, he was fast asleep.

~~~~~

It was pitch black by the time that Beau came to. He looked at his watch and groaned. It was just after midnight. Had he missed Molly? He jumped out of his truck again and sprinted up the sidewalk. As he rang the bell again, he looked at the cars parked in the complex. He still didn't see Molly's car, and it was also clear that no one was home. Where could she be? Had she gone on vacation with Macy? If so, they wouldn't have taken both cars to the airport.

Unsure of what to do next, Beau decided to head home and crawl into bed. He'd charge his phone while he slept, and then give Molly a call in the morning.

~~~~~~

Day shift was just getting started when Beau walked into the hospital at seven o'clock that next morning. He greeted a few of his colleagues as he walked by and told those who asked that his father was doing well, was out of the woods, and would be going home later in the week.

While Beau was relieved about his father's condition, he was starting to get really worried about Molly. When he called her this morning, it rang multiple times and then clicked into voicemail. He also drove by her apartment again on the way into work and saw that her car still wasn't there. After morning rounds, he decided he would give Macy a call and see if she'd been in touch with Molly. He hated to bother her while she was on vacation, but he didn't know what else to do.

Macy answered on the third ring. "Beau? Is everything okay? Am I needed at the hospital?" She hadn't expected to hear from him at all with everything that had happened with Natalie, so she figured the only reason he would be calling would be because of something work-related.

"Oh no, Mace. We're good here. I'm just calling because I haven't been able to get a hold of Molly for a few days. Is she with you in Texas?"

Macy paused, unsure of what to say. "No, Beau, she went back to Maryland. After everything that happened, she just wanted to go home."

"Everything that happened," Beau repeated. "What happened? Our fight about my dinner with Natalie?"

"She didn't care about the dinner, but she really lost it after you ran off with Natalie!" Macy didn't mean to raise her voice, but she couldn't believe Beau could be so naïve. Did he honestly think he could run off with his ex and no one would find out?

"Ran off with *who? Natalie?*" Beau's voice was raised now too. *What is Macy talking about?*

"Yes, Beau! Molly heard about you running off with Natalie. So she packed her bags and left town the other day."

"Wait a minute. Molly heard that? From who? Mace, I've been in Georgia for the past three days. My dad had another heart attack."

"He did? Beau is he okay?" Macy's voice grew serious.

"Yes, he's fine now, but it was touch and go there for a while. But tell me about Molly. What happened while I was away?"

Macy told him what she knew, which was when she left for Texas, Molly was completely over her fight with Beau and was looking forward to hashing everything out. Then Macy told him that the next time she heard from Molly, she had already left town and was a few hours from home.

"She said that she had stopped by the hospital that evening to surprise you with dinner. Then she was told that Natalie had been there, said she wanted to get back together, and you ran out after her."

"Who told her this?" Beau demanded.

Macy paused while everything sunk in. It made perfect sense. "Cassidy. It was Cassidy who told her."

~~~~~

Beau could not believe what Macy had told him. Cassidy had deliberately tried to sabotage his relationship with Molly. *Was she really that petty?*

Before he hung up with Macy, he told her the whole story. He told her that Natalie had come to see him and had wanted to get back together. He continued on, telling her that he told Natalie it was over for good and sent her on her way. It was only a few minutes later that he got the call about his dad and sprinted out of the hospital.

"I can't believe Cass would do this, Beau. I can't believe she'd sink that low," Macy said, stunned that her colleague would have acted like a silly school girl. She knew that Cass had had a thing for Beau, but she didn't think she'd take it this far. "I'm shocked that she'd do this to you – over a stupid crush."

"Well," Beau sighed. "I think it was more than a crush." He told Macy how he and Cassidy had gotten together occasionally, how, to him, it had been just a random hook-up. But it had meant more to Cassidy.

"This makes more sense then," said Macy. "I had no idea that you two had gotten together. But still – this doesn't excuse her behavior."

"I'll take care of Cass," Beau said. "Don't you worry about that. But in the meantime, please don't say anything to Molly. I need to be the one to straighten everything out."

Cassidy wasn't due to work until the following shift, but Beau was determined to speak with her and volunteered to work a double. When Cassidy walked around the corner and saw Beau standing by her desk with a somewhat menacing look on his face, she knew that he knew.

"I need to speak with you." Without waiting for Cass to respond, he turned and headed for his office.

After he shut the door, Cass exploded. "Beau, I can explain!"

"You can? You can explain why you deliberately lied to my girlfriend? You knew the truth about Natalie. I heard her say goodbye to you when she walked out of my office, and yet you still lied through your teeth. Why did you do it, Cass?"

"Because I thought if Molly wasn't in the picture, that you would choose me. I figured she'd leave town, and if you were upset, I'd be here to pick up the pieces. But I regretted it the moment I told her. I should have chased her down and told her the truth before she got in her car, but I didn't. I love you, Beau. I did it because I love you."

Beau paused for a moment, taken by surprise by Cassidy's confession. "You've got to be kidding me. Did you think I wouldn't find out? That Molly and Macy wouldn't talk? That all this wouldn't come back to you and your lies?"

Cassidy sighed and shrugged her shoulders. "I guess I had hoped that it wouldn't come out. I'm sorry, Beau. I really am. I'm ashamed of myself for behaving like that, but I couldn't help it. I did it out of love. It was my last desperate attempt to try and win you back."

"Win me *back?* Honey, you never had me to begin with." And with that, Beau stalked off, leaving Cassidy alone in his office.

~ Chapter 32 ~

It was three o'clock in the afternoon when Molly pulled up in front of her parents' house. Her dad was sitting outside on the porch that ran along the entire front of the house, rocking in one of their many chairs. He had been reading a book and smiled and waved as she parked.

"Hey there, sweetheart. Welcome home," her dad, Rick, said with a smile on his face. He was very happy to see his daughter and immediately pulled her close into a tight hug.

Molly hugged him back, taking in the smell of the cologne he always wore. Sometimes it was so nice for things to stay the way they've always been.

"Thanks dad. I missed you so much. It's good to be home."

Her dad held her at arms' length for a moment and looked her in the eye. "Is it? I hear you're coming home under less than wonderful circumstances. Do you want to talk about it?"

Molly shook her head. "Not really, dad. Not now. Thanks for asking though."

Her dad gave her a funny look. "Is that a stuffed fox you're carrying?"

Molly laughed. "It is – I bought him for mom in this small town outside of Lexington. I figured she'd like him."

Rick nodded. "Oh I can guarantee she'll love him."

Molly looked around. "Speaking of mom, where is she?"

"She's where she always is, down at the barn. She said to send you straight back as soon as you've arrived."

"Wonderful. I'll head there now. Thanks dad. And we'll catch up at dinner." She handed the fox to her dad so he wouldn't get dirty.

Her dad's eyes twinkled as he nodded in agreement. "Absolutely. Looking forward to it, Moll." He sighed for a moment. "It really is great to have you home."

Molly found her mother mucking out a stall and called to her from the top of the aisle. "Mom, I'm home!"

She heard her mother squeal and drop the pitchfork she had been using. "Oh those words are music to a mother's ears! Come here and let me look at you!" She practically catapulted herself out of the stall and sprinted up the aisle to greet her daughter.

The two women embraced. "Other than some tired, sad eyes, you look wonderful Molly. I'm so happy to have you home. You have no idea how much your father and I missed you. We wished you would have stopped by yesterday, but we understand you were exhausted from all the traveling the day before."

"I know. I wanted to come by, but I woke up yesterday feeling like I'd been hit by a bus. The day before had been *quite* a day."

While her mother finished mucking the stall, Molly filled her in on what happened with Beau. She felt her chin start to quiver when she described the scene at the hospital, with Cassidy telling her that Beau had just taken off after Natalie, but she steeled herself against her emotions and refused to let a single tear drop. She couldn't cry now, not in front of her mother.

Sensing her daughter's fragile state, her mother quickly changed to the subject to Gypsy by telling her that she'd prepared an empty stall at the end of the aisle for her so the horse could look out at the farm through the main door.

"I can't tell you how happy I am that you're getting another horse. It's going to be so wonderful watching you bring along another youngster. And Erin was talking about getting herself another horse as well. She thinks it would be fun to train with you and, how did she put it, 'bring your babies up together.'"

"That would be amazing!" Molly exclaimed. "We could even show together again, just like old times."

Molly helped bring the horses in for their dinner, measuring out the appropriate amount of grain for each. Molly noted with satisfaction that her mother had left no stone unturned when preparing Gypsy's stall. It already contained two water buckets, an additional bucket for grain, a salt lick, and a thick bed of shavings. It was perfect.

When the two women finished in the barn, they headed up to the house for their own dinner.

"I'm making your favorite tonight, chicken and dumplings," her mother said with a smile.

~~~~~

It was almost seven o'clock when Molly heard the van begin its ascent up her parents' drive. Gypsy was here!

Molly sprinted outside and directed the driver to the parking area down by the barn. He would have plenty of space to turn around once the horse was unloaded. Her mother and father were right behind her, anxious to meet their newest "grand-horse."

When Molly opened the side door to the van, Gypsy whinnied a massive greeting. "Hey girl! How was your trip? I bet you're tired. Let's get you out of here and into your stall." The horse playfully nudged Molly in the arm, clearly happy to see her mom.

The driver lowered the ramp and unhitched the chest bar. "Okay, here she comes," he called, and led the horse out the side ramp. Gypsy gingerly stepped out of the van and took a good look at her surroundings. A horse nearby called to her and she called back, happy to be off the van after the long haul east.

Immediately Molly's mom went over to Gypsy and stroked her nose, complimenting the horse on her good behavior. Then she began to remove her shipping boots and inspect the filly's legs for cuts or small injuries she may have sustained during her trek.

"She's very beautiful Molly, just like her new mother," her dad said, his eyes alight and dancing. "I can't wait to see you ride her."

"Same here," her mother chimed in with a smile. "She looks good to me. Legs are clean and cool – not even a scratch. And your father's right. She's breathtaking. You know how to pick them, my dear!"

Molly was beaming. Even though her heart was sad for Beau, it was bursting at the sight of her horse. This would be a new chapter of her life as an equestrian, and she had so many experiences to look forward to. She couldn't wait for her sister to meet her new baby, and the possibility of Erin getting another horse was absolutely thrilling. *Yes*, Molly thought, *everything is going to work out just as it should.*

~ Chapter 33 ~

Beau was reeling. He couldn't believe this had happened, that Cassidy had lied to Molly. She lied through her teeth when she knew damn well that Beau hadn't run off with Natalie. She may not have known where he had been running to, but she knew it wasn't after his ex.

After Beau had sprinted out of the hospital, he had called his supervisor, Roy, and told him of the situation with his father.

"No problem whatsoever, Beau. I'll alert your team that you've had a family emergency and will be out for a bit. Take your time. And I'll be praying for your dad."

Beau knew it was probably a matter of minutes before Cassidy and the rest of the team knew that he had left for Georgia. His father was lying in a hospital bed, he could have died, and Cassidy was back home, spinning tall tales to Molly. *It's a damn good thing I'm here at work*, Beau thought. And even here he was having trouble keeping his cool. He had had to walk out of his office away from Cassidy before he did or said something he would have regretted.

When Beau regained his composure, he went back to his office and called Molly. He doubt that she'd answer, but he needed to try and get in touch with her as soon as possible. The longer that she thought he'd left her for Natalie, the less likely he'd ever get her back. And he had to get her back – he knew now more than ever that she was the love of his life. Yes, he'd been with Natalie off and on for close to a decade, but now, after meeting Molly, after this summer, Beau realized what he and

Natalie had paled in comparison to his relationship with Molly.

Her phone rang and rang and then clicked over to voicemail. "Hi, you've reached Molly Sorrenson. Sorry I can't take your call at the moment, but please leave me a message. Thanks!"

My God I miss that voice, Beau thought to himself, heartbroken over what had happened. He felt sick thinking about the pain Molly must be going through.

"Hey sweetheart. Listen, I know I'm probably the last person on earth that you want to talk to right now, but I really need to speak with you. ASAP. I need to explain everything. Honey, it's not what you think – at all. Please call me back – day or night – I don't care what time it is. I love you, Molly."

Beau hung up and sighed. He felt truly defeated, and it was all because of Cassidy. Why did she lie? Why did Natalie have to show up? Beau felt like his life was spiraling out of control, and he was helpless to stop it.

Not knowing what else to do, he called Macy. She answered immediately.

"Hey Beau. What's going on?" She asked hurriedly.

"Well, I talked with Cassidy, and she admitted everything. Told me that she deliberately lied to Molly in hopes that we'd break up and she'd have another chance with me."

Macy was sympathetic as she could hear the hurt in Beau's voice. "Beau, I still can't believe it. I'm shocked she'd lie like that, but I guess I shouldn't be surprised. She's used to getting what she wants in life. Did you call Molly?"

"I did. She didn't answer. I left a message saying it was urgent that I speak with her, but I didn't go into detail. I don't blame her for not taking my call." Beau paused for a moment. "Mace, what am I going to do?" Macy could hear the strain and panic in Beau's voice. "I've lost her, and it's all my fault. I never should have taken up with Cassidy to begin with."

"Listen, Beau. This is not your fault. You didn't force Cassidy to *lie!* Look, I'll call Molly and talk to her. I won't tell her any of the details but will just say that she needs to take your call. Does that sound like a plan?"

"It does," Beau sighed into the phone. "Thanks Mace. I owe you one. I just hope that you can convince her to talk to me."

"I will. I'll let you know how it goes."

~~~~~

Molly looked down at her phone; she had a missed call from Beau. She listened to his voicemail and shook her head afterward. *He probably wants to explain why he chose Natalie over me*, she thought dryly. *No thanks.* She wasn't going to give him the satisfaction of listening to him, letting him ease his conscience while her heart continued to break. Let him feel like the dog he is.

She hated to admit how wonderful it had been to hear his voice though, and Molly loved Beau's voice. It was deep and strong and tough – just how a man's voice should be. *Stop it*, she scolded herself. She needed to stop thinking about him and get on with her life.

Molly had stayed with Gypsy until she was happily settled in her stall, munching on hay and looking out her window at the surroundings. She seemed perfectly content already; it was almost as if she knew she was home.

Home, sighed Molly. She was happy to be home too. Her tiny carriage house had never seemed more perfect. She had come back inside from getting her mail and was thinking just that when she saw the missed call from Beau. Tossing the phone on the couch, Molly steeled herself against the emotions rolling inside her and went into the bathroom to take a shower.

When she got out, she saw she had another missed call, this time from Macy, and she had left a voicemail as well.

"Hey Moll! It's Mace. I was hoping to catch you and talk because you need to know that there have been some misunderstandings with Beau and Natalie. He's going to give you a call later, and you *really* should hear what he has to say. No need to call me back – just answer when he calls, okay? I love and miss you. Texas is great, by the way. We should plan a girls' trip to a dude ranch out here."

Great. What's going on? Molly wondered. Although part of her was curious, she still didn't want to talk to Beau. There's nothing to misunderstand about a guy taking his ex back, for the second time.

~~~~~

Beau's phone chirped, and he looked down to see a text message coming through. It was from Macy:

Molly didn't answer when I called. I left a message saying that there had been a misunderstanding with you guys and to answer when you called again. Let me know if she doesn't pick up, and I'll call her again.

Thank goodness Macy is on my side during all this, Beau thought. He'd give Molly another call after he finished rounds.

Beau was just walking out of a stall when he ran into Marcus, the assistant trainer of Dawson Estate, who had come by to check on a horse who had been admitted the previous day with a minor injury.

When Beau looked up from his charts and saw him, he stopped and extended his hand. "Good to see you, Marcus. Guess you're here to check on Ransom; he's doing great."

Marcus shook Beau's hand and nodded happily. "That's great to hear, Beau. Thanks for taking such good care of our colt."

"No problem at all. How's Gypsy doing these days?" Beau asked.

Marcus slightly cocked his head to the side and looked confused. "Gypsy? She's gone. I watched her walk up on the van first thing this morning. She was shipped to Maryland, and belongs to Molly Sorrenson now. I figured you knew that."

So Molly had taken Gypsy with her.

It took Beau a few moments to shake his surprise. "Uh, actually I didn't know that. I've been out of town for a few days. Guess I missed quite a bit."

Marcus laughed and slapped Beau on the shoulder. "That girl. She's something else, meant business. She came up a few days back and said she was tired of waiting, needed an answer about Gypsy and needed to know that day. I could tell she was nervous as all hell, talking tough like that. But apparently the Dawsons had decided not to breed her after all, so the timing worked out perfectly."

Beau could picture that exact scene. Molly, fueled by her anger with him, marching up to Marcus and demanding the horse, all with her scared puppy dog eyes. She was tough in her own way and relentless about what she wanted. Beau smiled, secretly proud of her.

"Well, I'm glad to hear it worked out. I bet Molly was real happy."

"Oh she was," Marcus replied. "She started to cry, hugged me, hugged the horse. It was quite a scene."

Beau was sorry he had missed it, but even sorrier that he had caused it.

As soon as he was finished rounds, Beau ran back to his office and called Molly again. She didn't answer.

~ Chapter 34 ~

Molly's phone was ringing off its hook. Molly had just finished listening to Macy's voicemail when her sister's call came through.

"Hey, sis," Erin said through the phone. "Any chance you're up for meeting me for a drink tonight? We haven't caught up since you've been back, and I want to hear all about Mr. Cowboy Vet. So he turned out to be a dog, huh?"

Molly had to laugh. Erin had a way of saying things that was both heartbreaking and hysterical. There was something about her tone – it caught you off guard but was in no way malicious.

The last thing Molly wanted to do was rehash everything for Erin, but she knew she was going to have to at some point, and she *did* want to see Erin. She hadn't laid eyes on her sister since before she left for Lexington in June. It was almost nine o'clock, definitely not too late for a single girl to go out and have some fun.

"Yes," Molly laughed. "He was a dog. And I'll tell you all about it. Where do you want to meet?"

After solidifying their plans to meet downtown at The Canton Boathouse, Molly quickly changed out of her pajamas and into some jeans, heels, and a tight red sleeveless blouse. She didn't have time to dry her hair, so she tied it back into a low ponytail and was out the door.

~~~~~~

"Well, for someone who's just had her heart broken, you look pretty damn gorgeous!" Erin squealed when Molly walked through the door. The two girls quickly embraced.

"Oh Erin," Molly laughed. "You always know just what to say to make a girl feel special." She winked at her older sister, who looked pretty radiant herself. *It feels so good to be home with my loves*, Molly thought.

The two sisters ordered their glasses of white wine, and then decided to grab a table outside along the water's edge. When the waitress came over, they ordered a dozen blue point raw oysters.

"So, if it's too hard to talk about it, I won't press you, but I'm dying to know what happened. Wasn't it just last week that you told me you were staying in Kentucky for good? How did things go south so quickly?" Erin had a very direct way of speaking, but her eyes were sad and concerned for her little sister. Even though she had wanted Molly to come back to Maryland, she wanted her sister to be happy above all else. Even if that meant living two states away.

Molly sighed and shook her head. "You're right. This time last week I was ready to stay in Lexington for good, or at least past the summer, and maybe even move in with him. Can you believe it?" She was still stunned that everything had fallen apart so quickly. "And I wish I could say it was a long, sad story, but it really isn't. It was the classic case of going back to an ex."

Molly told Erin about Natalie, Beau's longtime on and off again ex, and how she had come to town to win him back. "When Beau met up with her and didn't tell me, it really hurt my feelings, but I wasn't going to break up with him over it, you know? We sparred a little at his house, and then I went home and vented to Macy. The next day, I was legitimately over it. Hell, I was bringing

189

him food at the hospital when I found out that he had chosen her."

Erin listened intently as Molly explained how she had missed Beau's call earlier in the day, and decided that showing up at the hospital with dinner was probably the best way to ensure them getting a chance to talk.

"And the next thing I know, Cassidy, another vet, tells me that Beau had just left the hospital with Natalie."

Erin shook her head in disgust. "So Natalie showed up at the hospital, told Beau she wanted him back, again, and he left with her? Just like that?" Molly nodded. "Wow, this girl must have some sort of magic spell over him. How ridiculous."

"I guess old habits die hard." Molly wasn't trying to defend Beau so much as figure out why he kept making the same mistake over and over. "What's that saying? Fool me once, shame on you. Fool me twice?" Molly started to laugh.

"Right?" Erin agreed. "Shame on Beau. But you know what? Better this happened now versus a few months from now after you'd have moved in and were all settled."

Erin had a great point. "I guess everything happens for a reason, and Beau and I just weren't meant to be." Molly was surprised that she had been able to recount the story to Erin without getting emotional once. *It must just be the wine talking*, Molly thought.

"Oh good, here come the oysters," said Erin, her eyes dancing. She reached across the table and put her hand on top of Molly's. "I really am sorry that Beau treated you so poorly, but I'm not sorry you're home!"

~~~~~

After Molly and Erin said their goodbyes, Molly decided to run to the restroom before she left the restaurant. Canton was probably forty-five minutes south of her home in Monkton.

While Molly was washing her hands at the sink, she smiled at herself in the mirror. Despite everything that had happened, she had been able to have a very nice time tonight and was glad she and Erin had gotten a chance to catch up. She was even happier to hear that Erin had definitely decided to get another horse and start competing again. She had taken a few years off from serious riding after she had gotten married and finished law school, but now the time was right. *Erin is way too good not to be in the show ring*, Molly thought as she dried her hands and walked out the door.

She took about two steps before a guy coming out of the men's room collided with her, knocking her sideways, her purse falling to the ground.

"Oh shit! Sorry, I didn't see you!"

Oh no, thought Molly. *That voice.*

"Molly? Is that you?" Ty asked as he reached out to steady her. "Shit, I'm so sorry. Are you okay?"

Picking up her purse and swinging it over her shoulder, Molly looked up right into Ty's eyes. He smiled that mischievous smile of his and gave her a once-over.

"Hey Ty," she said coolly. "Yes, I'm fine. No need to apologize."

His smile widened. "Wow, you look great. How have you been? Last I heard you were in Kentucky."

"Thanks, and yes, I was in Kentucky. I just got home actually, a few days ago. I was there for most of the summer."

"With Macy, I assume?" He asked. "Did you have a nice time?"

I can't believe I'm standing here making small talk with Ty. "Yep, with Mace. We had a great time together – it's beautiful out there. But the summer's basically over, so it was time I got back."

She paused for a few moments and then continued. "And what about you? The last I heard, you were about to become a father."

With that comment, Ty's smile faded, and he looked away uncomfortably. "Yeah, I am. She'll be here in another month. A baby girl. I'm going to have a daughter."

"Congratulations. And your…ah…girlfriend, she's doing well?" *Could this get any more awkward?*

"Well," Ty said with a shy smile. "Well, yes, she's doing fine, can't wait for the pregnancy to be over. But we're actually not together anymore."

"Oh!" Molly was actually quite shocked. "Sorry to hear that."

Ty looked around for a moment and then asked her if she'd like to grab a table outside and catch up for a bit. "It's been so long; I'd love to hear what you've been up to."

Molly hesitated for only the briefest moment. Ty, with his carefree ways, his dark and handsome good looks, was effortlessly gorgeous standing there in his jeans and black polo, his hair, longer than she remembered, looked a little windblown and tousled. She wanted to reach out and smooth it back into place, but caught herself. This was the man who had been her longtime love. But he was also the man who had been devastatingly unfaithful. Worse than Beau.

"I was actually just leaving, so I don't think so. But thanks. It was nice to see you. Tell your parents I said hey."

It was only after Molly got in the car and fastened her seatbelt that she realized she'd been holding her breath. Ty had enjoyed coming into the city often, so seeing him there hadn't been too surprising, but definitely unexpected. She was glad to hear he was doing well though. Even though he had behaved like a jerk at the end, she wished him the best of luck, and it sounded like he was going to need it.

Before she put her car in reverse, she looked at her phone. It had been on, but with the bustle of the restaurant, she hadn't heard it ring. She had three missed calls from Beau and one voicemail.

"Hi Molly, it's me again. Listen, sweetheart, I know you're mad at me, but I've really got to talk to you. Please call me when you get this. Please, Molly. I love you. I always have, and I always will."

Oh good Lord, thought Molly. *What could he possibly have to say to me?*

As she pulled out of the parking lot and began threading her way through the busy city streets to the I-83 exit, she dialed Beau's number and connected it to the Bluetooth. *Hell, this night can't get any weirder. May as well call him back.*

~ Chapter 35 ~

It was almost midnight when Beau walked out to his truck. His shift had been busy, but not overly so; still, he was looking forward to going home and hitting the hay, so to speak. He had just pulled out of the parking lot when his phone rang. Molly!

"Darlin'," he answered hopefully. "Is that you?"

"Hi Beau," Molly answered flatly.

Beau's sigh of relief was audible. "Molly, thank you so much for calling me back. I know you don't want to speak with me, but I really need to clear some things up. Do you have a few minutes to talk?"

"I wouldn't have called you if I didn't," she answered drily.

"Good, well, I'm not sure where to start, so I'll just start at the beginning, which I guess is the last time I saw you. I know I should have told you that I was grabbing dinner with Natalie and, honey, I was wrong about that."

"Beau, I told you when I left your house that I was basically over it. And, quite frankly, that is the least of my worries."

"I know, but you had a right to be upset, and the last thing I want is to sweep it under the rug. Anyway, I got called into work the following day, unexpectedly, and later that afternoon Natalie showed up. Told me she wanted to talk, and then she told me that she wanted to get back together. And, Molly, I told her that we were over, once and for all, we were through."

"That's not what I heard."

"I know. I know that Cassidy told you that I had left, that I had run after Natalie, and that is simply not true. Almost immediately after Natalie walked out, I got a call from my sister telling me that our father had had another heart attack. Molly, I flew out of there as if I was on fire and made it down to Georgia in record time." He heard Molly gasp.

"Oh my goodness, Beau! What happened? Is your dad okay?"

"He is, yes, by the grace of God he made it through. It was very serious for a while when he was in surgery and for twenty-four hours after, but he's goin' be okay."

Molly let out the breath she'd be holding. "Thank goodness, Beau. That's wonderful news." Molly couldn't imagine what Beau had gone through, receiving a phone call that his father might be dying. But wait, something didn't add up.

"Well, then why did Cassidy tell me that you had left with Natalie? Was she mistaken?"

Beau gave a soft, sad laugh. "Not exactly. Cassidy overheard Natalie telling me that she wanted to get back together, and she also saw Natalie leave a few minutes later. I heard them say goodbye to each other out in the hall."

"I don't understand then."

"Molly, Cassidy deliberately lied to you," Beau said. Molly was about to interject with another question, but he quickly continued on. "She lied because she was hoping you'd leave me and that she and I could get together. You see," Beau paused, sighing into the phone. "Before you came to town, Cassidy and I...well, we saw each other outside of work...occasionally."

"So you two dated?"

"Not exactly," Beau said. "It was more like a one-night stand that happened a handful of times."

"What you're saying, Beau, is that you screwed her when you felt like it. Am I right?" Molly sneered.

Beau sighed. "It only happened a few times, and I always made it clear that I never wanted a relationship, but I guess she had hoped for more."

"So you made it clear that you were just a love 'em and leave 'em kinda guy, huh? Real nice, Beau." Molly was stunned. Maybe Cassidy had lied and, yes, that was childish and sad on many levels, but none of this would have happened if Beau had just kept it in his pants.

But that's not fair either, Molly thought. Did she really think Beau had only ever slept with Natalie? That an attractive man like Beau just went back and forth from his house to the hospital every day without making time for a diversion here and there?

"Molly, I never meant to hurt her, and it was wrong of me to get involved with a colleague as well. But it just happened, and I feel terrible for hurting her the way I did. But you have to know, once I met you, I never thought twice about Cassidy, or Natalie for that matter. You're the one for me, sweetheart. It's always been you."

Molly's heart ached at those words. *Beau, I miss you so much.*

But wait – the kiss. "Cassidy told me she saw you and Natalie kissing. Was that a lie, too?"

"No, that part wasn't. Natalie did kiss me briefly goodbye. But that was it. One quick kiss before she left."

Molly didn't know what else to say, so she simply asked, "And how does Macy fit into all this? She called me earlier tonight."

"I kept driving by your apartment when I got home, and no one was there. I had no idea where you were, so I called Macy to see if maybe you had gone on vacation with her. She gave me a piece of her mind, as you can imagine, about how I treated you, and of course I had no idea what she was talking about. And then we realized that Cassidy was behind all this."

Molly sighed. "Beau, I really appreciate you calling and clearing everything up, but I'm not sure where this leaves us."

"This doesn't change anything between us. It can't, darlin'. I love you, more than ever, and I know that you still love me. I told Natalie that we were over for good, and Cassidy? Well, that was my fault, but you have to know that the last time she and I were together was before I even met you. I love you, Molly. Don't let this one misunderstanding ruin what we have," Beau pleaded.

Molly didn't know what to think. Beau had thrown a lot at her tonight. But how many more Cassidys were out there, waiting to come out of the woodwork and mess with their relationship? Could she really trust him again after all this? He lied by omission about meeting with Natalie, and then Molly had been an unwilling participant in high school drama with Cassidy. It was too much to take.

"Beau," Molly said sadly. "I'm already back in Maryland. And now that I'm home…I'm *home*."

"Not a problem," Beau said, not missing a beat. "I'll come to Maryland. I'm not going to lose you over this. I'll quit my job and move east."

"Beau, no, it's not that simple. Listen, I just need some time to process everything, okay? You've thrown a lot at me tonight and given me even more to think about."

"Look, honey, I know you've learned things about me tonight that you're not fond of. Hell, I'm not fond of them either, but you have to know. I'm not some cad who would pick up a different girl at the bar and bring her home. Yes, I've had a few nights like that, like the situation with Cassidy, but I'm a faithful man. I was with Natalie, and I have been with you."

"I know, Beau. I believe you." And Molly did. She was just reeling from the curve ball he had thrown her. "I just need some time. Can you give me that?"

"Honey, I'll give you whatever you need. Take all the time you need. I'm not going anywhere."

"Thanks, Beau. I'll call you when I'm ready to talk." And with that, she disconnected the call.

~ Chapter 36 ~

A full week passed and Beau still hadn't heard from Molly. He wanted to respect her and give her the space she requested, but he didn't know how much longer he could go on without talking to her. He had already cracked once and sent her a text message mid-week.

Just wanted you to know that I'm thinking about you – every minute of every day. I love you.

Molly hadn't responded.

"Are you sure about this, Beau? It seems awfully sudden," said Roy Jackson, Beau's boss at the hospital. "You've been here a long while now. I have to say, I'm pretty shocked."

Beau nodded his head. "Yes, I'm completely sure," answered Beau. "Roy, I've enjoyed working here more than you know, and I've especially enjoyed working for a great mentor such as yourself, but it's time for me to move on."

Last night as Beau lay in bed, he thought about his life, his options, and Molly, and the only conclusion he came to is that nothing else mattered if he didn't have Molly. He needed her in his life. So he came to the hospital the following day, his day off, to give his resignation, effective immediately.

"I'm sorry to be springing this on you with no warning," said Beau, "but I'm in a hurry to get to Maryland. And besides, I don't want to make a big deal about any of this."

Roy smiled and nodded. "So no going away party then?" He knew Beau's type. He was someone who wanted to fade into the night without any fuss.

"Right," Beau smiled back. "I'm going to make some rounds right now and say goodbye to whoever's here and then clean out my office. I'll send a hospital-wide email later if that's okay with you."

"Sure is," responded Roy. "And Beau?" He said as Beau got up to leave. "You always have a home here at Rood & Riddle. If whatever you have waiting for you in Maryland doesn't work out, we'd love to have you back."

Beau reached across the desk and shook Roy's hand. "Thanks, Roy. That means a lot, really does. I appreciate all you've done for me over the years."

~~~~~

A few hours later, Beau was almost finished cleaning out his desk when Macy stopped by.

"Hey stranger," she said as she knocked on his open door. "If I had known that I was coming back to bad news, I would have stayed in Texas!" Even though her tone was serious, she had a smile on her face. She knew what Beau was doing.

Beau walked around his desk and greeted Macy with a hug. "I was hoping I'd get to see you in person before I left," Beau said, grinning like a kid in the candy store. Now that he had given his resignation, everything was official. He was going to Maryland to be with Molly. Molly didn't know that yet, of course, but that was his plan. He wanted to surprise her.

"I spoke with Molly earlier today, and she didn't mention that you were moving. Am I correct in assuming that she doesn't know about your upcoming change of address?"

"You are correct, Mace. I'm going to surprise her. How she handles it, well, that's to be determined."

"Wow, Beau, that's mighty brave of you, don't you think? Quitting your job and moving east before you've run everything by your sweetheart." Macy was almost one hundred percent sure Molly would take him back, but she also knew Molly and knew that she hated surprises.

"I want to show her how serious I am. There's a difference between telling her on the phone that I'll quit my job for her and showing up at her house having already done so."

"When's the last time you spoke with her? Are things getting better at least?"

Beau laughed a little. "We haven't talked in over a week. She said she needed space and, hell, I wanted to give it to her, but I just can't. I need to be with her, Macy, and I won't take no for an answer." Macy had never seen Beau look so serious.

"Well, for your sake, and your career's, I hope you two can work things out. Molly hates surprises though, so don't be shocked if you show up to a less than friendly greeting on her part!"

"At this point, Mace, I'm prepared for anything," he said with a grin. "Just do me a favor and don't tell her I'm coming."

"Even though you know my loyalties lie with Molly, your secret is safe with me. I'm really going to miss working with you, but I'm not too sad. I have a feeling that we'll be seeing each other for the rest of our lives." And with that, Macy gave Beau yet another hug and left.

~~~~~

The sun was already starting to set when Beau threw his bag in the back of his truck and put the key in the ignition. He was getting a late start.

It took him a little longer than he'd expected to say his goodbyes at work, and then he had stopped in to see the Richardsons. They were sad to hear that he was ending the lease on his house, but assured him that they'd take care of Ace until Beau arranged to have him shipped east. Beau would be back for the rest of his belongings, so for now he threw some clothes and a toothbrush in his bag and sped down the road. It was after seven o'clock by the time he left, late enough that he probably should have just waited until the following day to leave, but once he had made up his mind to go, he didn't want to waste a single minute.

When he had spoken to Macy earlier, she had told him that the drive was going to be at least eight hours. That would put him arriving on Molly's doorstep in the middle of the night, and he couldn't do that. Beau would drive as far as he could, grab a hotel room for a few hours, and then hit the road bright and early.

Since it was after rush hour, traffic had eased up along the main highways, and Beau was able to make great time as he drove east out of Lexington. He was pretty exhausted, but the thought of reuniting with Molly fueled him on.

Two hours into his journey, he stopped at a gas station to fill up and made himself a large coffee. Ideally, he hoped he could make it through all of West Virginia and into Maryland before he had to stop for the night. He had never been to West Virginia, so Beau was a little disappointed that he'd do most of his traveling in the dark and wouldn't be able to see the scenery around him. *But that didn't matter*, he thought to himself. All that mattered was getting to Molly as fast as he could.

Beau had to admit that he was pretty nervous about how Molly would react when she saw him. The last thing she had said to him was to give her some space, and what was he going to do? Show up on her doorstep a week later with news that he had left his job and given up his home, for her.

She'll either hug me or strangle me. One or the other, or maybe both, Beau thought with an anxious laugh. He knew he had his work cut out for him.

Beau had never encountered so many twists and turns and hills and valleys as he had in West Virginia. It wasn't an easy state to drive through, especially late at night and as exhausted as he was. It was just after one o'clock in the morning when Beau crossed into Maryland, found a small hotel in Garrett County, and booked a room. He set the alarm for six o'clock, just a few short hours later, and fell asleep on the bed without even changing.

After the alarm sounded, Beau was up, showered, and in his truck within twenty minutes. He still had a ways to go, and he was anxious to see Molly and clear the air.

Before hitting the road, he stopped to grab a quick breakfast and coffee. After that, it would be smooth sailing right into Baltimore County.

~ Chapter 37 ~

The sun was shining through the curtains when Molly began to stir. She glanced at the clock and saw that it read seven-fifteen. Impressed with herself for getting up before her alarm went off, Molly rose and stretched. She wasn't surprised that she had risen early today. The previous day had been exhausting, and she had fallen asleep by nine o'clock that night.

She and Gypsy had had their first ride together, and it had been perfect. The little filly was everything Molly could ask for: affectionate, kind-hearted, and willing. Molly had started out slow, just walked Gypsy in the outdoor sand ring adjacent to the barn, and the young filly had handled it like a pro.

After the ride, Molly had spent the rest of the day around her parents' farm helping with chores and hanging out with Gypsy, watching her graze in one of the paddocks. Erin and Kevin came over in the evening for a family dinner, and Molly beamed like a proud parent when Erin exclaimed that Gypsy was the most perfect girl she'd ever seen.

It had been wonderful to have the whole family gathered around the dining room table again. And it was then that Molly told everyone about her conversation with Beau the previous week.

"So he was running out to be with his sick father, not his crazy ex?" Erin asked. When Molly nodded in affirmation, Erin continued. "Sounds like a pretty reasonable excuse then, Moll. Are you taking him back?"

"I have no idea what I'm going to do," Molly said honestly. "I asked him for some space for the time being so I could think everything through." And while she had been thinking about her future with Beau, she still didn't know what that looked like.

"Well as long as you don't go back to Kentucky, I don't care what you do!" Molly's mom said with a laugh.

Molly, smiling to herself as she remembered her mom's very typical reaction, meandered into her tiny kitchen, desperate for her morning cup of coffee. She drank it outside on her patio and watched the world come to life around her. When she was younger, dusk was her favorite time of day, the time when the lightning bugs would come out, flashing up the backyard and the tree-line beyond it. She loved that happy, tired feeling of a day well spent and would go in for a shower only after she'd said goodnight to all the horses, planting kisses firmly on their velvet noses.

But now Molly was falling in love with early mornings on the patio with her steaming cup of coffee, the birds' wake up calls to one another, and the anticipation of another day unfolding. Molly smiled to herself at this realization. *I must be getting old*, she thought. *Maybe I'm not as much of a night owl as I thought.*

~~~~~

Beau sat in a little rush hour traffic just outside the town of Frederick, Maryland, but within twenty minutes he was moving again and made pretty good time from that point on. When he saw the sign welcoming him to Baltimore County, he sighed with relief. He was almost there.

Macy had given him Molly's address, but told him that she lived in a carriage house just beyond the main house. She also said that Molly had her own driveway that was unmarked and easy to miss. As Beau wound his way through the back country roads, he slowed his speed so he wouldn't make a wrong turn.

Molly wasn't kidding when she said she had lived in the middle of foxhunting country. While Beau was used to driving by massive, immaculate horse farms, this area had a slightly different, unique charm. There were coops built into the fences, allowing horses and riders to jump from pasture to pasture while out riding to hounds. It also seemed a little hillier than Lexington, and the views around each bend were spectacular. There was something classic about it.

The GPS on his phone showed that he was just a few minutes away.

~~~~~

After her morning coffee and breakfast on the patio, Molly dressed for the day. She was having her local vet, Dr. Elizabeth Adams, out that afternoon to give Gypsy a good once over and exam. Molly wanted to see if Dr. Adams had any suggestions for the young filly's training program, especially given her history with the bowed tendon.

When Molly had ridden her the day before, it had been a very light ride, just walking around the perimeter of the ring. Despite her age and her recent injury, Gypsy had felt fairly balanced and connected, but Molly wondered if acupuncture or massage therapy would help ease her into her new exercise regimen. Dr. Adams would be able to make some good recommendations.

She planned to spend most of the day over at her parents' house, helping around the farm. Molly threw her Kindle in her purse, grabbed her car keys, and walked out the door.

~~~~~

Beau found Molly's place easily, and made a right turn into the driveway and followed it around to a small parking area in front of an adorable house. It was all stone and probably well over one hundred years old. He noticed that ivy completely covered one side of the house giving it the look of a sophisticated cottage, but Beau also noticed that there wasn't a single car in the driveway. If Molly was home, he figured he'd see her Ford Explorer.

He got out of his truck, walked up to the front door, and knocked loudly. As expected, there was no answer. Not knowing what else to do, Beau peered into the closest window and saw a room that appeared to be an office. Books lined a built-in bookshelf and he saw pictures of Molly, some with various horses, and some with, he assumed, friends and family members. He definitely had the right address.

Beau walked around the sidewalk that led to a small stone patio. It had a table and four chairs, as well as a couple flower boxes filled with blooming Black Eyed Susans, the Maryland State flower. The view from the patio was breathtaking as it overlooked rolling acres of horse pasture. Molly had been right; the carriage house had been a perfect place for her to call home.

But, clearly, she wasn't home. Beau didn't want to bother her again, but he picked up his cell and called Macy. She answered on the second ring.

"Hey Beau, how's everything going?" She asked breathlessly. He could tell that she'd been waiting for either him or Molly to call with some news about their reunion.

"Hi Mace. It's not going so well. I just pulled up to Molly's, and she's not here. Any idea where she'd be? Should I just wait here?"

Macy was quiet as she thought for a moment. "I bet she's at her parents' farm. She's probably spending some time with Gypsy or just helping her mother around the barn. I don't remember their address, but I can tell you how to get there from where you are now. If you make a right out of Molly's driveway, you'll make the first right at the next street, Monkton Road, and then you'll make a left onto Carroll Road. Their farm is about a mile down on the right, and you'll see a green and white sign that says *Misty Maple Manor*."

"Got it," Beau said with a nod of his head. "I'll head there right now. Thanks Mace, you've been a huge help."

"No problem, my friend. And good luck."

~~~~~

Though its arrival signaled the official end of summer, which Molly found upsetting, she had to admit that September was probably the best month of the year. The weather was perfect for riding as the humidity had finally relented, and it was dry unlike the rainy months in spring.

She hadn't planned on taking a morning hack on Traveller, but she couldn't resist. The sun was shining, the temperatures were in the mid-seventies, and Trav had been standing patiently at the gate.

Molly had smiled when she saw her old friend eagerly waiting for her, and she thought again how stupid she had been to consider leaving him behind if she moved to Lexington. Even though Traveller was older, he still loved getting out for an easy ride through the trails. Within fifteen minutes, she had tacked up her horse and they headed out.

She let Traveller have his head and they walked peacefully through the worn path. Unlike Kentucky, the trails here weren't as smooth and wide; they were a little rocky in some places, but her faithful gelding had no trouble navigating this familiar territory.

Molly knew that Trav probably hadn't been ridden since she had left for Kentucky in June, so the ride would be on the shorter side, but she'd try and take him out regularly to build up his stamina.

Eventually, Molly made her way out of the trails and Traveller walked briskly in the bridle path between two fence lines. As they crested the top of a small hill, Molly noticed a man leaning against the fence of Gypsy's paddock. The filly had come over to him and was sniffing his face and rubbing her head on his shoulder. *Who is that?* She wondered.

As she got a little closer, Molly inhaled her breath sharply. With his long, lean body, simple plaid shirt, and green John Deere baseball cap, she recognized him at last. "Oh my God," she said aloud to Traveller. "It's Beau."

~ Chapter 38 ~

When Beau pulled up in front of the old farm house that had been beautifully restored and maintained throughout the years, he saw Molly's car. He bounded up the wide wooden plank steps and rang the doorbell. No answer. *She's probably down at the barn*, he thought to himself.

He peeked into the barn and saw that it was deserted. Where on earth could Molly be? Then he heard a familiar whinny and saw Gypsy galloping up to him. His heart burst with happiness when she saw that the filly had clearly recognized him. She looked the picture of health; she was as sound as could be as she danced on her long, slender legs.

Beau jogged over to Gypsy and took her head in his hands. "Hey girl! Let me look at you." He immediately scratched behind her ears, and the horse leaned into his caresses. "You look perfect, you know that? And you have the best mama in the world now. I'm so happy she got you."

The horse shook her head briefly and began rubbing her head on Beau's shoulder. He couldn't believe how much he had missed this filly. She truly was something special. *And now*, Beau thought, *she belonged to someone equally as special.*

Gypsy abruptly stopped rubbing and turned her attention to Beau's left. She nickered softly as a horse and rider came into view at the top of a small hill. Beau's heart leapt in his chest. He had found Molly at last.

Molly was riding a grey horse and based on her previous descriptions, Beau guessed it was Traveller, her old hunter. She pulled the horse up in front of Beau and he noticed instantly that Molly's eyes held a mix of emotions, and he couldn't quite get a read on her.

"Hey Beau," she said quietly. "What are you doing here?"

He cleared his throat and smiled up at her. "Molly, we need to talk. I know I said I'd give you some space, but I just…I needed to see you. Can you spare a few minutes?" He asked hopefully.

Molly couldn't believe he was here, that he'd driven all the way from Kentucky to see her. "Yes, we can talk. Just give me a few minutes to untack Traveller and turn him out." She squeezed with her legs and urged the horse forward. She dismounted at the entrance of the barn and walked inside.

Beau turned his attention back to Gypsy who was waiting patiently for some more scratches. He fished in his pocket and pulled out a peppermint. Gypsy's ears perked up at the sound of him unwrapping the plastic and gobbled up the treat as soon as Beau offered it.

Molly exited the barn a few minutes later, led her horse down the walkway to one of the nearby pastures, released Traveller, and hung his halter and lead rope on a fence post. Then she turned to Beau and squared her shoulders, steeling herself for the conversation ahead.

"My father is at work and my mother is at an appointment, so the house is empty. Would you like to come up for a cup of coffee?" She asked somewhat wearily.

Beau nodded. "Yes, I'd like that very much."

They walked into the tastefully decorated house and into the large, country kitchen. It was painted a light yellow and Beau thought that the brightness must reflect the happy family that resided within.

Molly turned on the coffee pot and busied herself gathering two mugs, creamer, and sugar. She sat everything down on the island that was positioned in the center of the kitchen and waited for the coffee to brew.

As she filled the mugs, she spoke to him without looking up. "So what brings you to Maryland, Beau? I assume you weren't just passing through." She carried the mugs over to the table, and they sat down across from one another. Beau noticed that Molly's hands trembled slightly as she clutched her coffee mug.

Beau's eyes held so much emotion that Molly feared he was about to cry. "Oh Molly," he began. "I'm so sorry for everything that's happened. Darlin', I love you so much, you know that, don't you?" Molly nodded. "I know that you asked for space, and I'm sorry that I couldn't give you more than a week of it. I had to see you. I have to be with you."

Beau reached out and took Molly's hands in his. "You're going to think I'm crazy," he went on, laughing ruefully, "but I quit my job." Molly's eyes widened, and she drew her hands back away from Beau's.

"You what?" She asked incredulously. "Why would you do that?"

"Because I'm moving to Maryland to be with you. Please tell me that you'll have me."

Stunned, Molly didn't know what to say. Had he really quit his job?

"Listen, Molly, I know we still have some things to work through, but I know there's no one else for me. I know the whole situation with Natalie and Cassidy was a fiasco, but that's all behind us now. Let's start fresh, here and now. I'll start my own practice here. Hell, I don't care where I work or what I do as long as I'm with you. If you need more space still, that's fine. I'll grab a hotel nearby, but I'm not leaving," Beau said firmly. And then he smiled weakly, "You're stuck with me."

When he finished, Molly had tears in her eyes. She wiped them with a napkin and then took a sip of her coffee, as if trying to buy some time and decide what to say. Over the past week, she had been leaning more and more towards getting back together with Beau, but she knew the distance was going to be an issue. Now that she was home, she didn't want to go back to Kentucky. But Beau had just removed that problem from the equation. Now she could stay home *and* have Beau.

Not knowing what to say, she asked, "How's your dad?" Beau smiled and told her that he was doing just fine. His dad was home and getting stronger every day.

She smiled. "That's very good to hear. I'm sorry you had to go through all that alone. I wish…I wish I would have known." She wiped her eyes again and looked up at Beau sadly. "Beau, I don't know what to do. I love you, and I'd love for us to be together again, but I can't let you give up your life in Kentucky. Your career, the life you've built there, it's all just too important."

"It's too late," Beau said with a wicked grin. "I told you, I already quit. I'm here to stay. And besides, nothing is more important than you, and I can't imagine my life without you."

Molly started to cry again.

"And to be honest with you," Beau continued, "with all that's happened with my father, I've been thinking it's time for a change anyway. It's made me realize that being with my loved ones, well, that's all that matters in life. Besides," he said with a mischievous grin,

"I bet Ace would love it around here. He told me he's had enough of that Kentucky bluegrass."

Molly laughed at that. She couldn't believe what she was hearing. Everything was working out better than she ever could have hoped. Beau rose, walked around the table, and pulled Molly to her feet. Holding her chin in his hands, he bent down and kissed her as passionately as he could, and she wrapped her arms around his neck and returned his kiss with everything she had. The love of her life had returned and was here to stay.

~ Three Months Later ~

"Get down from there," Beau called. "Let me do it." Molly was attempting to balance herself on a rocking chair to place the angel atop of their Christmas tree. She was still a few inches shy of reaching.

Beau picked her up and held her in his arms. "Let me do it, shorty. You're goin' to hurt yourself," he said with a smile. He gave her a gentle kiss on the forehead as he helped her to her feet.

"I do this every year without you, you know," Molly responded playfully.

"Well not anymore," Beau replied, easily placing the angel at the top. "I'm here now," he said with a wink.

And it was true. Shortly after getting back together, Beau returned to Kentucky and packed all of his belongings, and in true bachelor fashion, he had very little. A few books and a chest of drawers full of clothes, and that was it. The move into Molly's carriage house went seamlessly.

Ace made the journey to Maryland as well, and now lives with Gypsy at Molly's parents' farm. Molly's family, of course, was overjoyed that she decided to stay in Maryland, and they already love Beau like he's part of the family.

The only unhappy person is poor Macy who is still in Lexington. "Not cool, Molly," she said jokingly over the phone when Molly called to tell her the news. "It's bad enough that you decided to go home, but now you're taking my closest friend at work with you? You are a terrible best friend," she said with a laugh. "I'm just kidding, of course. You know I couldn't be happier for you two!"

Molly hoped that one day her best friend would return home as well. But in the meantime, she had Beau and the equine love of her life, Gypsy, to occupy her time. Gypsy was maturing into a perfect little lady, like everyone knew she would. She would be turning three in mid-January, and Molly couldn't wait to start training her over fences later in the coming year. The horse was a true athlete and brave as could be. It looked like Molly found her eventing partner after all.

When they had finished decorating the tree, Molly and Beau turned off all the other lights in the house so they could better admire their handy work. The little tree glowed and twinkled, its white lights sparkled bright.

"Aww," Molly said, wrapping her arms affectionately around Beau. "Our first Christmas tree. Isn't it beautiful?"

"It sure is," Beau agreed. "We should celebrate all our hard work," he said with a playful look in his eye.

"Celebrate?" Molly asked, playing along. "How?"

Beau scooped her up in his arms and carried her toward the bedroom. "I have an idea."

Molly threw her arms around Beau's neck and laughed. She was so grateful to have spent the summer away, only to have returned with a renewed appreciation for her home. And she was even more grateful to have found such a wonderful love along the way.

~ Acknowledgements ~

A tremendous ***thank you*** to everyone who helped shape this novel into what it is today.

To Kay Yeager, Kim Gerhardt, Helen Parker, Mary Miller, and Susan Moyer – thanks for being my proofreaders! You all did a phenomenal job editing various drafts, and I truly appreciate your time and effort.

To Dr. Cecilia Garrett, DVM – thank you for being my "horsey" expert.

To Clara Abdurazak – you have always been in my corner, forcing me not to settle for anything less than the best, and motivating me to do what makes me happy. Thank you for being my "wisdom!"

To Nicole and Kenny Dorsey – you two were more instrumental than you could ever know. Not only were you wonderful editors, but your positive attitudes, plot and theme suggestions, thought-provoking questions, and constant encouragement kept me going when I wanted to throw in the towel. I'm honored to call you both my friends – "thank you" isn't quite enough. Can't wait for the script!

And finally – to James. Even though I may have given you dirty looks every time you asked, "How's that book coming?" I secretly appreciated it. Thanks for always pushing me in the right direction, even when I try and dig my heels into the ground. You are my biggest supporter and my best friend. I love you!

~ About the Author ~

Laurie Berglie lives in Harford County, Maryland, with her husband, James, and their seven four-legged kids. She enjoys renovating her fixer-upper farm, reading horse books, and training and competing her two OTTBs, Misty, her wild mare, and Bailey, her easygoing gelding. She has a BA in English from Stevenson University and an MA in Humanities from Towson University. This is her first novel.

For more information, please visit:
www.laurieberglie.com or her blog at
www.themarylandequestrian.com.

You can also find her on Instagram @marylandequestrian.

If you liked this book, please consider writing a short review on Amazon or Goodreads! They help so much and mean the world to us self-published authors. Thank you!

Made in the USA
Columbia, SC
07 July 2020